CW00570682

A *Love Match*
FOR THE
Marquess

CARA MAXWELL

Chapter 1

"Did it go well?" The young woman asked in an excited whisper as she hurried up the wooden stairs.

"I don't know, they've only just arrived!" The man in front of her said over his shoulder, hastily adjusting his livery as they reached the top of the stairs. He paused before opening the door, modeling taking a deep breath in and out, hoping the young maid would do the same. But she was breathless with anticipation, her eyes dreamily imagining the royal court. The footman, who was not much older than the woman, felt a small smile turn up the corners of his mouth. "Here we go," he said before quietly opening the door and stepping into the long foyer of the townhouse.

At the other end of the mansion, a neatly clad butler was opening the heavy front door and the housekeeper was standing at attention ready to greet the family. Mrs. Miller bobbed a curtsy as a short, plump woman entered, followed by a formally dressed middle-aged man, and finally, a young woman, dressed in head-to-toe white satin.

"It went perfectly!" Anne Hutton announced to the house at large, her voice booming through the marble hallways. "Just perfect! She was a complete success. All of the other debutantes were clearly jealous of her, and all of their older brothers were clearly interested. An unequivocal success!"

"That is splendid, my lady," Mrs. Miller, the housekeeper, said with a genuine smile as she took the lady of the house's reticule, gloves, and hat.

"Now don't go overboard, my dear," Anne's husband chastised from behind her, where he was handing his overcoat and hat into the waiting hands of Hux, the butler who had traveled with them from Sommerfield.

"Are you saying it did not go well?" Anne said, her pitch rising a few octaves.

Harold took his wife by the arm and patted her hand affectionately. "It went well enough, indeed," he agreed. But then he cast a meaningful look over his shoulder, where their daughter stood removing her own outerwear. "But don't forget, Madison is a force unto herself."

Madison rolled her eyes, removing her elbow-length white satin gloves and handing them gratefully to the housekeeper. Mrs. Miller rewarded her with a knowing wink. Since the family did not usually spend time in London, they had brought their household staff from their estate at Sommerfield to the townhouse they had rented for the duration of the London Season. For not the first time, Madison was grateful to have familiar faces around her now.

The household staff: maid, footman, butler, and housekeeper, all smiled at her indulgently. The young lady of the household represented them all and they were quite attached to her. She made an impressive picture in her all-white ensemble. Her satin gown was intricately embroidered with little flowers across the sleeves and bust. A line of tiny jewels encrusted the neckline, and a peek of lace showed just above her bosom to ensure the perfect amount of modesty.

"It all went to plan." Madison acknowledged with a gracious smile. Dressed in her specially made gown, arranged just so, she had been presented at court and was now ready to officially enter the social whirl of the London *ton*. "There were perhaps some young men who looked interesting. But of course, I am not going to settle. I know what I am looking for."

"You are looking for a husband." Anne reminded her succinctly.

"I am looking for the right husband." Madison retorted.

Anne threw up her hands in exasperation, a little wobble of annoyance tremoring through her rounded frame. "What am I going to do with her?" She loudly asked the room. The servants kept their eyes carefully averted, well used to Lady Sommerfield's flair for the dramatic. Madison knew better than to ruffle her mother any further. It was almost like a well-rehearsed scene was playing out, one that the family had enacted a hundred times. Madison said something controversial, Anne had a big reaction, and right on cue, Harold swooped in to bring his wife back down to earth.

Harold reclaimed his wife's hand and tucked it neatly into the crook of his arm. "Come along, my dear. Let's have a spot of tea to calm your nerves," he said with complete sincerity. His soothing voice faded away as he led his wife out of the foyer and into the drawing room.

Madison watched her parents fondly as they walked into the drawing room, her mother chattering on and her father chuckling warmly. She shook her head, smiling to herself. What a pair they made, her mother and father.

Without thinking about it, she reached up and started removing the pins that held up her long blonde hair, setting them absently on the marble table next to her in the foyer. *That* was what she wanted, she thought to herself. Her mother was absolutely right; the reason they were in London this season was to find her a husband. But not just any husband. A peerage, a fortune – those things mattered greatly to her mother, but they were immaterial to Madison. While some young women set their caps on the rakes and rogues of London, hoping that they would be the ones to win them over and make them change their stripes, Madison wanted nothing of the sort.

What she wanted was exactly what she'd just watched up close; what she had been watching up close for her entire life: a love match. No rakes or rogues for her; a kind, laughing, and most importantly, a loving gentleman was what she sought.

Racing along the lane, Henry did not dare glance back over his shoulder. He could hear the other rider behind him, coming up on his right flank. If he looked back, even for a second, then he would give up his advantage and surely be caught up. Without conscious thought, he tried to urge his mount faster: gripping her sides a little harder with his knees, leaning forward on her glossy brown neck, loosening his grip on the reigns ever so slightly. The willing mare took his cue and dug in, finding a last reserve of speed. Henry could feel the smile beginning to spread on his face; he was almost there.

Suddenly, he felt the heat and movement of another body on his right, and the other horse and rider pulled in line with him. Henry tried to urge his horse forward, but she had used her reserves and couldn't keep up as the others surged ahead of them. They whipped past the tall oak tree at the side of the lane, and both riders eased up, slowing their mounts to a canter and then a trot.

"Why the hell are we riding two hours outside of London to look at a horse? You already have all the best ones." Henry said with an exasperated grin as his and Theodore's mounts finally came abreast of one another.

His friend rewarded him with a slight smile. "Taking the loss particularly hard today, are we?" Theodore said.

Henry laughed. "If the race had ended fifty yards before the oak, I would have had you," he contended.

"If that is what you need to tell yourself." Theo slowed his horse to a walk, and Henry did the same alongside him. "Anyways, you could do with losing every once in a while. You are a little too used to getting exactly what you want," Theodore added.

"I always seem to lose to you on horseback." Henry reminded his friend. "But next time I have you for a round of cards or billiards, I am going to show you what it feels like to lose."

"You can give it a go at the club tonight," Theo said.

"Actually, I am unavailable tonight," Henry said, fiddling with his reins as they guided their horses down the well-worn road.

Theo looked over at his friend in surprise, asking his question without having to say it aloud.

"I am attending a ball being given by Viscount and Viscountess Herrin this evening," Henry explained.

Theodore pulled up on his reins in surprise, startling his horse. Bringing the animal in hand, he shot a curious look at Henry. "A ball? Not your usual evening entertainment. Is one of your sisters in town?"

"God, I hope not," Henry said with mock horror. "Denise and her family came down to London last season to launch her eldest daughter, Louisa. But now that Louisa is married and off in Exeter, I don't expect to see my sisters. At least not until much later in the spring," he clarified. Theodore was still looking at him in confusion, his question unanswered.

Henry sighed, shaking his head with a little smile. *Well, best be out with it,* he thought to himself. "The Season is officially underway. If I am going to find a suitable wife before midsummer, I need to start looking now. Logically, it makes sense to start meeting the women soon, before too many of them have found their matches and are off the market, so to speak."

Theodore looked completely gobsmacked. Unable to find the words to speak, he looked away from his friend.

He stared at the spot between his horse's ears, an inscrutable look on his face. Henry did feel a little bad taking his closest friend by surprise. They had been mates since they met at Harrow when they were teenagers. They had been friends long enough for Henry to know exactly how his friend felt about marriage; it was not exactly favorable. But all of that aside, he also knew that if he was going to undertake this endeavor, he would need his friend at his side. Henry was the sole son in his family line, his parents deceased, and his elder sisters thankfully all far from London.

Trying to lighten the mood, Henry reached over and jabbed Theodore in the side. "Are you alright there, man? A marquess in the market for a wife is not exactly groundbreaking." Henry joked.

Theodore did not smile, but he did seem to break out of his trance. "That is true," he allowed. "But you have not talked about this before. Where is this coming from all of the sudden? Are your sisters putting pressure on you?"

Henry shook his head. "Have I ever let my sisters pressure me into anything?" He said with a laugh. "We've done it all, my friend: fought our teenage brawls, lost embarrassing sums at the card table, worked our way through the bordellos of the Continent. It just feels like its time; time to find an amenable bride, and have some heirs."

He could see Theodore shaking his head, clearly not able to wrap his mind around what his friend was saying. But Henry was not bothered. He had been thinking about this ever since the end of the last Season. Last year, he had spent an obscene amount of time escorting his sister and niece around, providing the protection and gravitas of his status as a marquess. It had opened his eyes and reminded him that while he had enjoyed a long and independent bachelorhood, he could not live that way forever. He had responsibilities to his family, his estates, and his title. Spending more time at *ton* social events this season was not high on his list of enjoyable leisure activities, but it was the best way to accomplish his goal. Just as he had told Theodore: he had made his rounds as a rogue bachelor marquess, now it was time to find a wife.

Chapter 2

*S*tanding on the side of the ballroom sipping her punch, Madison tried to melt into the wall. While she had always enjoyed a party, she was finding herself a bit overwhelmed right this moment. This was her first London ball. The first time she had been out, in society, as a fully-grown woman. She had been dreaming about this for months … nay, years. And though she had anticipated that she would get on well – she was used to being the center of attention – this was an experience even she was not prepared for.

The room seemed to glitter, illuminated by candles and mirrors that reflected and intensified the light. There were easily two hundred guests in attendance, and when those masses were reflected by the mirrored walls it seemed like a thousand. Tall pillars painted gold held up two-story-tall ceilings, which were themselves adorned with intricately painted murals. Madison's home in the country was comfortable, her parents were very well off and they lived in a luxury not enjoyed by most country-based nobility. Madison had attended many dances, dinners, musicales, and teas at the homes of the surrounding gentry. But none of it compared to the crush and shine of London. It was brilliant and exhilarating, and Madison was totally dazzled.

As she took another fortifying sip of punch, she glanced at her dance card. Her *full* dance card. Madison had barely stepped into the ballroom before she was approached by a young man asking for a dance. And then another. And another. Her mother was positively aglow with joy. Madison's optimism was more guarded. Her card may be full ... but was it full with the right kind of man? Was her future husband's name somewhere on the list tied to her wrist, unbeknownst to either of them?

Madison bit her lip to bring herself back to reality. Perhaps there was something alcoholic in this punch, she thought to herself. It would not be long before the dancing began; she could see the musicians setting up in the corner of the ballroom. They looked like they were almost ready to start.

As if on cue, a young man of middle height approached Madison. Her first thought was that he looked more like her brother than her suitor; their hair was the exact same shade of golden blonde. Repressing that ungenerous thought, Madison forced herself to smile. She searched in her memory, trying to summon up his name from the long list of introductions she'd received in the last hour.

"Miss Hutton, I believe they are about to play our song," he said smoothly, cutting a crisp bow and offering his hand to Madison.

"Indeed, they are, Lord Green," Madison said with a polite smile, accepting his hand. She congratulated herself for remembering the appropriate address, but could not for her life recall his title. However, she was spared any awkwardness because as soon as the music started to play, he began to talk about himself.

"A ball is not my normal entertainment. My father, the Earl of Westerley, had to attend to a last-minute parliamentary issue, and of course, as a gentleman, I could not leave my mother unescorted," Green said, putting a not-so-subtle emphasis on his father's title. Madison did not roll her eyes, but it was a testament to her self-control.

"How lucky I am that you have graced us with your presence," she said with only the slightest hint of exaggeration. A shadow of doubt flickered over Lord Green's face; he was not quite sure if she was being genuine or facetious. Arrogant man that he obviously was, it was hard for him to fathom a young debutante being anything less than impressed by his title and self-importance.

Over Lord Green's shoulder, Madison saw her mother watching them attentively. With great effort, Madison forced back the next sarcastic comment she had ready and spoke more genially instead. "Are you very interested in your father's politics, Lord Green?"

He frowned. "Indeed, Miss Hutton. It is my duty as the future Earl to stay apprised of the current issues. But I hardly think this is appropriate talk for a young woman."

"Why not?" Madison said sweetly, the challenge confined to her expressive hazel eyes. The future Earl's own eyes widened. He clearly did not expect to be questioned by a young woman. He probably expected her to flutter her eyelids, look away demurely, and mutter some nonsense like *"Whatever you say, my lord."*

"Women have no place in politics." Lord Green said definitively, his dander rising.

"Women live by the laws that Parliament passes, do we not?"

"Yes, but —"

"Then it stands to reason we most definitely are entitled to an opinion, at the very least," Madison said smartly, her lips pursed.

The future Earl was no longer sputtering. He was peering down at her with clear disapproval. The song came to an end, and he delivered her to the edge of the dance floor without pause. "Good evening, Miss Hutton," he said, dipping a perfunctory bow before beating a quick retreat into the crush of partygoers.

Good riddance, Madison thought to herself as he disappeared. Her father was right, she reflected. She had made a good first impression on the *haute ton*, but once these one-dimensional suitors got to know her, their ranks were bound to thin out. Well, that was fine with her. Madison was not interested in a man who thought his title was the most important thing about himself, or who thought she should be a demure wallflower without opinions. She wanted someone who would see her, all of her, and appreciate it. A counterbalance, a partner. Just like her parents, she reminded herself. *On to the next*, she told herself.

Sure enough, a dark-haired gentleman was approaching her through the crowd as the first notes of the next dance sprang forth. Fixing a smile on her face, Madison waited to greet her next suitor.

"He seemed quite taken with you!" Her mother said excitedly. Anne's plump figure was adorned in dark rose-colored silk, her graying blonde hair neatly pinned up, perfectly matching ruby earrings and necklace in place. She was of a height with her daughter – which was to say, not of much height. She shared her daughter's boisterous demeanor; they both tended to call attention to themselves, though their energy was distinctly different.

"Quite taken with my bosom is more accurate," Madison said sardonically, watching the retreating back of her third dance partner of the evening.

"Madison! Do not be vulgar!" Anne exclaimed, putting her hand to her chest as if she might faint.

"None of these men are right," Madison said, hearing the sound of defeat in her voice.

"None of these men are right?" Her mother repeated hollowly. "How can you say such a thing? You've only just met them. My goodness, what about Lord Green, he is the heir to the Earldom of Westerley!"

"And he made sure I did not forget it." Ignoring her mother's alarmed look, Madison reached for a sweet from a passing tray. She ate it slowly to avoid having to say anything more to her mother, who continued to look around the room in exasperation, opening and closing her mouth like a fish.

Feeling a little bit bad for her mother, Madison resigned herself to consulting her dance card to find out her next foe. While she and her mother might have different criteria for selecting an appropriate husband, if she wanted to meet the right man she would probably have to meet plenty of wrong ones. "Alright, mother –"

"Maddie!"

Madison was engulfed in a cloud of burgundy taffeta as her friend Eve burst through the crowd, giving her an excited hug. "I am so glad to see you! I was so cross with David for not letting us come to London sooner. I cannot believe I missed your presentation at court!"

As she was speaking, Eve reached over and grasped Anne's hand, leaning forward to quickly touch cheeks with Madison's mother.

"Eve – Lady Brockton," Anne corrected herself. "You never fail to make an entrance, my dear," she observed with raised eyebrows.

Eve smiled mischievously. "That is why my mother had me married off last season. She could not risk me making a fool of myself a minute longer."

"She was probably right," Madison said with a grin. "Mother was most glad that we would not have the opportunity to get into mischief together."

"You two are incorrigible." Madison's mother said plainly.

"Do let me steal her for a moment, Lady Sommerfield? I promise I am a respectable *ton* wife these days," Eve asked. Anne looked the two young women over, clearly skeptical, but she knew when to pick her battles. Eve was not her favorite of her daughter's friends, but she had managed to make a respectable marriage last season. Maybe she could bring Madison around.

"I am going to the ladies' retiring room. Do not forsake any of the kind gentlemen who have requested a dance," Anne said, giving her daughter a pointed look before departing.

"Have you already had lots of interest?" Eve snatched the card at Madison's wrist, a wide smile growing on her face. "Maddie, your card is full already!" She exclaimed with a delighted giggle.

"Eve, these men are terrible." Madison shook her head, reaching for another passing petit four. "The first one, future Earl of whatever, was completely self-obsessed. The second one, well … to be fair I am not sure he understood half of what I was saying. Not exactly a razor-wit, if you get my meaning. How did you ever find David amid this mess?"

Eve gave her friend's arm a sympathetic squeeze. "You are right. Finding a man worth your time in the London *ton* is like digging through coal trying to find a single diamond. But when you find him…" Eve's eyes lit on her husband, who was talking to a small knot of other men. A warm smile lit her face. "I will just say that the right one is worth the wait." A very becoming flush washed over Eve's face and chest.

Madison watched her friend with undisguised envy. Eve had found her match. If she could do it, so could Madison. She pulled her dance card back out and reread the names listed there. Maybe he *was* there somewhere.

Chapter 3

"*L*ord Warsham! What a lovely surprise!" Viscountess Herrin fell on him like a hawk upon its prey. The middle-aged woman, the host of the evening's event and mother of two unmarried daughters, was not about to let the eligible marquess pass her by. He was not a frequent guest at events like these; indeed, he had a reputation for more disreputable haunts.

"Good evening, my lady," Henry said smoothly, offering her a charming smile.

"When I saw your card returned, I was most pleased! It is not often that we entice you to one of our little gatherings." The lady smiled self-indulgently as she drew him into the main ballroom. The floor was teeming with guests dancing, conversing, and drinking.

"When I saw your invitation among all the others, I could hardly refuse. Your 'little gatherings' have a big reputation," Henry said, allowing her to lead him. The Viscountess blushed, looking very pleased with herself. No doubt, her next move would be to introduce him to her daughters. Henry felt an instinctive clench in his stomach but reminded himself that this was why he had come tonight. To secure the perfect wife, he needed to first meet her.

"Tell me, are your sisters joining you tonight? We so enjoyed having them down to London last season." Viscountess Herrin asked, quite obviously trying to ascertain the reason behind his unexpected appearance. She was leading him through the crowded ballroom, walking with a clear destination in mind.

"I am afraid not. I do not expect them until much later in the Season, if at all. My entertainments are my own, this evening." He emphasized the last sentence just slightly, but it was enough for the perceptive lady to catch his meaning. She looked like she might burst with excitement. Finally, the marquess was in the market for a wife.

"Well, then, it is my duty as your hostess to ensure that you are well looked after," Viscountess Herrin said, her voice brimming with glee. "Lord Warsham, may I introduce you to my daughters, Harriet and Imelda."

"You are *too* kind," Madison said, accepting the glass of champagne.

"You are an excellent dancer, Miss Hutton," the young man said. He barely looked old enough to be out of the schoolroom. He was annoyingly earnest, but at least he was not ogling her bosom or stepping on her toes. Overall, he was an improvement on many of the gentlemen she had met this evening.

"Thank you, I have had a lot of practice this evening," she said, trying not to let her exasperation show.

"Would you like a rest? I am sure I can procure us a seat somewhere?" He said, looking around quickly.

"No, no, I am quite alright." Madison patted his arm, trying to calm him like an overexcited animal. "I see my dear friend Lord Bowden just over there. It would be impossibly rude of me not to go say hello. Will you excuse me?"

The fresh-faced lord looked crestfallen, but to his credit, he smiled and nodded. "Of course, Miss Hutton. I hope we can talk more later!"

Madison fought back the urge to chuckle as she smiled and walked away. He really wasn't that bad, but he certainly was not her true love. Maybe in four or five years he would make someone very happy. Madison filed that information away; if her younger sister ever returned from Paris, perhaps she would introduce them.

As she weaved her way through the throngs of people, she acquired another flute of champagne. "Good evening, Christopher," she said, handing him the glass without waiting for a reply.

"Madison." Christopher accepted the glass, taking a sip as he surveyed the crush of guests. "I see you are interested in adopting a young puppy," he said without looking at her.

"Ha!" She laughed aloud. "If you can believe it, that sweet young gentleman was the best prospect I have met so far this evening."

"I do believe it," Christopher said quite seriously.

"This is going to be much harder than I thought," she mused aloud.

"You are usually the darling of parties like this. What are you complaining about now?"

"Now, now, Christopher, don't be rude." She elbowed him in the side. "That is not what I meant. I do love a party," she admitted. "But when one has a goal other than just frivolity, it does take the pleasure out of it a bit."

Christopher glanced over at her. He had known Madison for a long time. To someone who did not know her as well as he did, she looked perfectly composed. Her long golden blonde hair was perfectly coifed. Her silver and diamond jewelry, no doubt borrowed from her mother, perfectly accented her aquamarine gown. She looked like a petite, perfect princess. But above her clear hazel eyes, her brows were furrowed.

"Alright," Christopher sighed. "What are you worried about?"

"Why Christopher, is that concern I hear in your voice?" She teased.

"Never mind –"

"Alright, alright, I am sorry," she said, patting his arm. "Every man I meet is just so … wrong."

"Wrong?" Christopher asked.

"Too pompous, too superficial, too young," Madison gestured back towards her last partner. "How am I supposed to find a husband among this lot?"

"Lower your standards, clearly." Christopher took a deep drink of his champagne.

"A man I can love, build a partnership and a family with…that isn't asking too much, is it? At this point, just a man I could stand being around for more than five minutes would be an improvement." Taking a hint from Christopher, Madison drank a deep gulp of her wine.

"That is your first mistake, Madison. Thinking that love has anything to do with all of this." He shook his head at the crowd dispassionately.

Madison pursed her lips and looked up at Christopher, considering. "Love doesn't have to hurt, Christopher," she said quietly.

She watched his knuckles tighten on his glass, turning white with tension, and knew she had gone too far. No, Christopher's heart was not ready yet to broach that topic. "Never mind," she said quickly, pointing them back to the crowd *en masse*. "Is there anyone you think I should consider?"

"Not especially. I usually don't pay much attention to the male contingent." As he said it, his eyes caught and followed a suggestively dressed woman who looked to be in her early thirties. Not a debutante whose reputation he could spoil, Madison thought thankfully.

"I admit, I was a little surprised to see you here tonight," she said, spotting her mother and father in conversation with another middle-aged couple across the room. She felt a modicum of relief; her mother was occupied and would probably leave her alone for the time being.

Christopher cleared his throat beside her. "I had to get in one night of entertainment before I leave for Spain."

"Spain? In the middle of the Season?" Madison asked with surprise.

"I am looking into acquiring a factory in Barcelona. Unlike you, I do not see the Season as a reason to stay behind." Christopher was only half-listening to the conversation, continuing to make eyes at the other woman. *Lord, please let her be a widow or something*, Madison prayed quickly.

Sighing, Madison filed Christopher's revelation away. She would not be able to rely on him to hide from her bevy of odious suitors. It was just like him to run away in the middle of the Season; if one wanted to avoid love and marriage, best to stay far away from match-minded debutantes and their mothers. Keeping one eye on Christopher's lady of interest, Madison looked again over the full ballroom.

Over the heads of almost everyone else in the room, a new figure caught her eye. The man was very tall, easy to spot amid the tangle of nobility. His light brown hair was a unique shade; not quite blond, but shot with bolts of gold amid the darker mahogany brown. And he was laughing. He had a brilliant smile. Madison felt her stomach do a little flip.

"Who is that?" She said, poking Christopher in the arm to get his attention.

Clearing his throat in a sound of annoyance, Christopher rolled his eyes but followed her gesture. His eyes immediately narrowed. "The tall bloke?"

"Yes, standing with Viscountess Herrin's daughters," Madison confirmed.

"Lord Warsham, Marquess of Clydon."

Madison caught his tone. She looked up at Christopher with interest. "Do you know him?"

"We are members of the same club." He said shortly.

"Excellent! Then you can introduce me!" Madison said with a bright smile. She hooked her arm through Christopher's and started to step forward.

"Absolutely not." Christopher refused to move, causing Madison to stumble. She shot him an irritated look.

"What is it now? I finally find a gentleman who looks interesting and you will not introduce me? Some friend you are," she said with annoyance.

"I said we were acquainted. That does not mean I like the man."

"I see." She crossed her arms and looked at him expectantly, awaiting further explanation.

"He thinks he is better than everyone else. Looking down his nose, literally. Too damn tall, it is unnatural," Christopher muttered.

"No actual reason I should not meet him, then. Thank you for your help," she said sarcastically. She tossed back the small remainder of champagne in her glass and then handed it to Christopher. "Since you're going to be abandoning me to jaunt off to Spain, I think it's only fair that I abandon you to make the acquaintance of the Marquess of Clydon. Good evening, Christopher."

"Yes, I have spent a fair amount of time in Scotland. My father had holdings there. I find the countryside to be quite beautiful, especially the Highlands. Though the residents can be a little surly when they realize you're a Londoner," Henry explained in answer to Harriet, the elder daughter of Viscount and Viscountess Herrin. The group of young women that Henry was speaking to had grown slowly over the past half an hour. Originally, it had been just Viscountess Herrin's two daughters and himself. But then a friend of Imelda, the younger sister, had come along to greet her and had lingered.

A few minutes later Lord Brenton, an acquaintance of Henry's from Harrow, had appeared with his sister on his arm. And on it went. He was introduced to a young woman, they exchanged a few empty pleasantries, and the circle around him grew.

Henry glanced over the heads of those around him, an advantage of his height, and confirmed what he suspected: the group was getting sidelong glances from other guests. Others were watching and whispering with interest. The secret of his eligibility was out and it was already the talk of the ball. *Well, at least this was an efficient way to go about it*, Henry thought to himself.

"That is so interesting, Lord Warsham. I would love to visit Scotland myself," Harriet said with a pleasant smile. She was a pretty girl, Henry had to admit. And she had cleverly kept herself at his side since her mother had delivered him to her despite the growing interest of the many debutantes in attendance. "I hear –"

"Pardon me, you are Lord Warsham, is that right?" A clear, confident voice interrupted Harriet.

Henry turned around in surprise, following the voice. Its owner was a petite blonde young woman, whose curtsey in front of them made her even seem even smaller. When she stood up and tipped her face up towards his, her smile was radiant.

"Indeed, I am." Henry managed to say. Did he know this young woman from somewhere? He looked at her closely, noting her high-cheekbones and slightly larger than normal hazel eyes. He did not recognize her. "Have we met, my lady?"

"Miss Hutton. Miss Madison Hutton. My father is Baron Sommerfield. I do not believe we have met before, my lord," Madison explained, her smile unwavering. Then she turned her eyes to Harriet. "Harriet, darling, I am so sorry to interrupt you. You must think me unconscionably rude. Do forgive me?" Madison stepped forward and laid an imploring hand on the other young woman's arm, artfully inserting herself into the center of the group.

Harriet, of course, had no other recourse but to mutter a *"Not at all"* politely, as the daughter of the host. Madison did feel a bit bad about out-maneuvering Harriet, who was a sweet girl. But this was the first gentleman Madison had been interested in all evening and she was not going to miss her chance to meet him. With that, she turned her attention back to Henry.

"My dear friend, Lord Bowden, mentioned that you were familiar. I was so interested to make your acquaintance I am afraid I've left him behind." She glanced over her shoulder to where Christopher was still glowering across the room.

Henry's eyebrows shot up at the mention of Christopher Bowden. 'Familiar' was a kind word for their acquaintance; in fact, he was unsurprised when he followed the young woman's gaze and saw the other man glaring at him. Nonetheless, he was interested in Miss Hutton. It was highly unusual for a young woman to approach a gentleman and introduce herself. Usually if one of them was interested, they must find a mutual friend or connection to make the introduction. That was just the way it was done. Henry was intrigued by a woman who would buck all of those norms without blinking an eye.

"I do not think you could have dragged Lord Bowden over here unless you had a cattle prod, to be honest," Henry said with a chuckle.

Madison rewarded him by widening her smile. "Ignore him," she said flippantly. "I certainly try to."

"You are a wise young woman."

"Would you mind telling that to my mother? She is of a decidedly different opinion."

Henry laughed, and Madison felt a wave of warmth course through her. Dear Lord, he was handsome when he smiled and laughed like that.

"Where is your mother, Miss Hutton? Is she well? I do not believe I have seen her this evening." Harriet interrupted, attempting to insert herself back into the conversation.

"She is quite well, thank you." Madison felt her heart thumping wildly in her chest as she turned toward Harriet. Perhaps it was better to look away from Henry for a few moments. She was afraid her heart might burst out of her chest if it started beating any harder. "I meant to tell you, Harriet, that the dress you wore for your presentation at court was exquisite. The beading, the lace…I admit, I was quite jealous," Madison said sincerely. Harriet blushed pink at the compliment and her face softened into an appreciative smile.

"You look very beautiful this evening, Madison. Your necklace is lovely." Harriet returned the compliment.

"Thank you, it is my mother's. I am surprised she trusted me with it, it is one of her most prized possessions," Madison joked.

"Are you known for losing things, Miss Hutton?" Henry asked, clearly amused.

"Not usually," Madison responded, meeting his warm brown eyes for the first time. Then she was distracted by something over his shoulder. A stout gentleman in a steel gray waistcoat was approaching through the crowd. "Except tonight it appears I have lost track of the time. I see my partner for the next dance approaching."

Henry caught her hand and opened her dance card. "You are quite popular this evening, Miss Hutton," he observed as he flipped through the pages, finding them all filled.

"I am afraid so," Madison answered, her breath catching in her throat. His fingertips on her wrist sent jolts of energy up her arm, straight to her heart.

Glancing over his shoulder Henry saw the approaching gentleman, a man he vaguely recognized, about to join the group. Without pause, he crossed off the name for the next dance and wrote his own. Madison's eyes widened in surprise, her mouth dropping open.

Henry turned to the other man with an apologetic smile. "I am sorry, my friend, but I simply must have this next dance for myself." And without pausing to wait for a reply, Henry took Madison's hand and led her onto the dance floor.

Madison was so shocked she could hardly contain her nervous chuckle. But it died on her lips when Henry put his hand on her waist, pulled her close, and started to waltz with her. She felt like all the air had been forced out of her lungs. She was literally breathless.

Henry looked at her curiously. "Did I do wrongly? Would you have preferred I left you to dance with that gentleman?" He asked honestly, trying to read her emotions.

Madison shook her head. "No, not at all," she said quickly.

Henry felt himself relax noticeably. He realized how disappointed he would have been if she had answered differently. He also realized how nice she felt in his arms. She was much shorter than him; he was tall and she was petite. But when he started to dance with her, somehow, she fit his embrace perfectly.

"You mentioned you saw Miss Herrin when she was presented at court. I can only glean from the full dance card that you were presented yourself, and it must have been quite a success," Henry said. He was acutely aware of the curve of her hip where his hand was placed. How much of that was her dress and how much was the woman beneath, he found himself wondering.

"I think the greatest victory is that the whole thing is over," Madison said with a grimace. "I was so nervous. I admit I was excited to come to London for my first Season. But an audience at the royal court…no thank you."

"You are an unusual woman," Henry said honestly. Madison bit her lip to keep from laughing.

"I am not sure if that is a compliment or not," she said, her chest rising with suppressed mirth.

"Certainly a compliment," Henry clarified, giving her hand a conspiratorial squeeze. "Most young women of my acquaintance cannot wait to be presented at court."

"Well, I am not like most other young women," Madison said directly. Looking up at him, she found herself caught in his gaze. His rich brown hair had fallen over his forehead, casting a slight shadow over his dark, warm brown eyes. Before they had been laughing. But as they met hers now they were filled with an intensity she did not understand but was instantly attracted to.

"You most definitely are not," Henry said softly. The music was trailing off, the dance ending, but they were still standing in the middle of the room. People were beginning to stare at them. Henry knew he needed to release her. It was completely inappropriate for them to be standing in the close embrace of a waltz like this for so long. But he did not want to let her go.

Madison took a deep breath. In her periphery, she saw her mother watching from the edge of the dance floor. She glanced over, breaking their gaze. As if a spell had been broken, Henry released her and stepped back. He cleared his throat.

"Miss Hutton, may I call on you tomorrow?" He asked, his voice thick.

Madison nodded. "Yes, I would like that very much," she managed to say. Henry bowed to her, nodded to her mother, who was approaching from the side, and then departed through the crowd. Madison dug her fingernails into the palms of her hands, trying to convince herself that the last fifteen minutes had been real.

"That was the Marquess of Clydon," her mother said, coming to stand beside her daughter.

"Yes," Madison breathed. She did not know if this feeling raging through her veins was love, but it was certainly a start.

An hour later, Henry sat down in a thickly upholstered leather chair next to Theodore. Nursing a drink, Theo was watching a game of billiards.

"How did it go?" Theodore asked without shifting his eyes away from the game.

Henry sighed, crossing his arms contemplatively. "I think I may have just met my future wife."

Chapter 4

*H*enry awoke early the next morning. Theo was not available, so he went for his morning ride alone. He took full advantage of the lack of patrons at the park at this early hour, riding hell for leather through the long, deserted lanes until both he and his mount were panting for breath. He pulled out his pocket watch to check the time. It was still too early.

Still bursting with energy, he dismissed the groom that came forward to take his horse when he entered the courtyard of his London house. Instead, Henry tended to the animal himself: walking him out until he was fully cooled, brushing out his coat and mane, and finally rewarding him with a hearty breakfast back in his stall. Then he headed back inside the house.

As he entered his study, he could not stop his gaze from going to the ornate grandfather clock that stood in the corner. Still too early, he told himself. He rang for tea and sat down at his desk. There was a stack of social invitations. He flipped through them, but they did not hold the same interest that they had even yesterday. Because he had already met the woman he wanted.

"Thank you," Henry murmured to the maid who brought in the tea service: a steaming pot of tea, cold cream, and a tray of scones. He smiled. They had not even bothered to include sugar on the tray because they knew he never took it in his tea. How did Madison take her tea, he wondered? Perhaps his staff would have to change their habits. He found himself smiling at the thought.

He prepared his cup and sipped it with satisfaction. He could not have imagined a better start to his search for a wife. At his first ball, he had met a woman who was confident, beautiful, and intelligent. Madison checked all the boxes on Henry's list. The next move would be to initiate a formal courtship with Miss Hutton. Henry mused about what that would entail.

Once the hour was decent, he would call on her today as promised. He should bring a gift for her mother. *Good*, he thought to himself, *that would help him fill the time between now and when he could reasonably call.* When he did arrive, he would need to speak with Madison's father and formally express his interest. There should be no doubt in any of their minds what his intent was. He was no longer a rake looking for entertainment. He was a marquess in search of a wife.

Then perhaps he would invite the family to his residence for tea. It would allow him to get to know them all a little better in private, away from the prying eyes of London society. Her father would be able to see his daughter's future home and assure himself that she would be well provided for. Her mother would be duly impressed and wooed, which was essential to winning any young debutante. He had learned that last summer with his sister and niece. After that, he and Madison would need to be seen walking out together socially. After various instances of being seen together in public – *say three*, Henry reasoned – he would formally propose.

He drank the last of the tea and ate one of the scones as he thought through the particulars. He did not have parents to play host for him and his sisters were far from London. He would be responsible for orchestrating this whole endeavor himself. But that was fine. Henry was used to doing things on his own. And the prize was Madison. He felt a flush of desire wash through him. Yes, the rush of attraction he had felt for her was a promising sign as well. Not required for a successful marriage, but it would certainly make the production of heirs all the more enjoyable.

Checking the clock a final time, Henry called for his coat and headed out to put his plan into action.

Madison told herself she would not look at the clock on the mantle of her bedroom until her maid left the room. She forced herself to sit still while the young woman brushed out her long blonde hair, but when she started to plait it Madison stopped her. "No, I think I will wear it loose today."

The maid raised her eyebrows. Naturally, everyone in the household had heard that the young mistress was expecting a caller of consequence today. Madison's mother had overheard Henry's promise, which she had then related to Harold, Madison's father. And they had of course discussed it as they took an evening cup of tea after arriving home, which ensured that the entire household staff knew exactly why both female members of the family were on edge this morning.

Wearing one's hair down and loose was decidedly out of fashion, and also generally made young women look more child-like, which was not the impression most wanted to make on a prospective husband. But Madison did not care. She did not like having her hair pinned into tight coiffures. It gave her a headache. And she felt her hair was her best feature. It was an unusually vivid golden blonde, and it reached well down her back and shoulders. She allowed her maid to pull it back at her temples and weave a sprig of baby's breath into the back, but that was all.

Madison dismissed the maid as soon as the young woman's hands set down the hairbrush. The instant she heard the door click, Madison's eyes flew to the glass-encased clock on the mantle. Ten in the morning. It was still too early for Lord Warsham to call. Only family and close friends would call in the morning. Other social calls were reserved for the afternoon. She knew if she went downstairs, her mother would drive her insane. Madison resigned herself to spending the morning upstairs avoiding her mother. Sighing, she rang for tea and a newspaper to keep her occupied.

She did wonder what Henry would think of her morning habit of reading the newspaper. Most young women were taken up with the local society papers or scandalous romance novels. Nothing so erudite as news and politics. Madison shuddered thinking of the deplorable Lord Green. She certainly knew what his opinion would have been. Having always been her father's darling, Madison had spent many a day playing on the floor of his study while he worked. It was there she had found the morning's discarded news, and as she learned to read, the interest held within. Her mother had given up trying to break her of the unladylike habit. Would Henry be similarly put off? *I hope not,* Madison found herself thinking as she stirred a bit of cold cream and sugar into her steaming hot tea. And if he was, well, he probably was not the right gentleman for her. But the usually brash young woman did find herself saddened by that thought.

At twelve noon, Madison descended the stairs of the townhouse her parents had rented for the Season. While not as familiar as her parents' manor house at Sommerfield, it was equally comfortable and perhaps more upscale. Madison suspected her mother had chosen it because she wanted to make a favorable impression on any gentleman callers. Madison's father was a baron, the lowest-ranked member of the nobility. But even for that, her family was far from destitute. Her father's smart business investments and well-managed estate meant they were better off than many of the less prudent earls and viscounts that frequented the London social whirl. Since Madison's younger sister Meera had run off to Paris with their great aunt, Madison was the only remaining daughter. A fact which Anne reminded her daughter of on an almost daily basis. To say she was eager to make the right impression and see Madison well-married was a gross understatement.

Anne was waiting for her in the foyer, wringing her hands nervously. "Are you ready?" Her mother asked.

"It is early yet. It could be hours before he comes to call," Madison said practically, though she was just as excited and anxious as her mother.

"He was quite interested yesterday evening," Anne said enthusiastically. "Crossing off Lord Hammer's name on your card and writing his own … why, all of the ladies were talking about it."

Madison could not help smiling. It was true; Lord Warsham had made quite an impression. She forced herself to take a deep breath to try and get her wild nerves under control. She motioned towards the open doorway off the entry hall. "Mother, perhaps we should go and wait in the sitting room –"

They were interrupted by a loud, firm knock on the front doors. Both their eyes flew towards the sound and then back to each other. Anne swiftly grabbed Madison's hand and started pulling her towards the sitting room. "Come along, we must not appear overeager. Let Hux bring him to us."

Henry waited outside while the Hutton's butler presented his calling card. For a moment, he wondered if there was a possibility his visit might be rejected. Perhaps he had misjudged the situation. After all, his interaction with Madison last night had been brief. Brief, but electric. No, he reassured himself. A woman who was bold enough to cross a ballroom and introduce herself was not the type to play games and turn him away.

The door opened again. "Lady Sommerfield and Miss Hutton are happy to receive you in the sitting room, my lord," the butler said, welcoming him into the house. Henry glanced around, noting the stylish furnishings and well-dressed staff as the butler guided him into the sitting room. Madison had mentioned her father was a baron, Henry remembered. The family appeared to be remarkably well-off for a barony.

Madison's mother jumped to her feet the instant that Henry entered the room. But Henry's eyes went immediately to Madison, who was standing at the front windows framed by the early afternoon sunlight. She was dressed demurely, in a light pastel green appropriate for a debutante, embroidered with flowers along the neckline. Long tendrils of her blonde hair clung to the neckline of her gown, drawing his eyes to her breasts. Her chest was going up and down heavily, his only indication that she was as exhilarated as he was.

Anne cleared her throat, drawing his eyes back to her as she curtseyed formally. "Good afternoon, Lord Warsham. We are most pleased to welcome you," she said.

Henry inclined his head. "Thank you for seeing me, I know it is a little on the early side of the day," he said politely.

"Not at all!" Anne insisted. "Please, please sit with us. Madison?" She beckoned over her daughter, but Madison was already crossing the room, perching on the edge of the sofa. Henry sat next to her.

"Miss Hutton, you look radiant this morning," Henry said honestly. Madison smiled and let out a small laugh.

"You are quite the charmer, Lord Warsham," she said candidly. Her mother looked horrified, but Madison ignored her. "I do thank you. I see you have your hands full." Madison nodded to the packages he was holding.

"Yes, of course." He handed the first parcel to Madison. "These reminded me of you, Miss Hutton."

Madison pulled apart the loosely wrapped paper to reveal a small spray of daffodils. She was touched by the simple gift. Most men she knew would have purchased a large, showy arrangement designed to impress. Henry's complete lack of guile was disarming. She also could not imagine a kinder comparison than to the sunny, bright flowers that heralded the arrival of spring. "Thank you, Lord Warsham," Madison said sincerely, smiling up at Henry.

Henry wanted to lean over and kiss her. Her lips, curved into that enticing smile, were calling him. Shaking himself free of the impulse, he turned to her mother and handed her the other package, a rectangular parcel wrapped neatly in white paper.

"For me?" Anne said, a little surprised and a lot pleased. She accepted the parcel, carefully unwrapping it. Inside was a small leather-bound book. As she opened it, she saw that it was filled with a collection of expertly pressed flowers. "This is lovely, Lord Warsham. I am most moved."

"I am glad you like them, Lady Sommerfield. I believe the flowers are native to the area of your family seat," he explained.

"What a thoughtful gift," Anne said. "You have thought of everything, my lord."

"I admit, Lady Sommerfield, that I do have one more item I hope to accomplish while I am here. Would Lord Sommerfield be willing to grant me a few minutes of his time?" Henry said smoothly.

Madison felt her stomach lurch. He wanted to speak to her father. That could only mean one thing:

a formal courtship. Anne looked like she might burst with joy. Madison did not feel far off from it herself.

"Of course, I am sure he can accommodate you. If you will excuse me for a moment, Lord Warsham, I will speak to him." Madison's mother stood and hurried from the room, her excitement evident.

"Well, you have certainly made her day," Madison said as soon as her mother was gone.

Henry laughed at that. "I hope so. But she is not the only one I am hoping to impress," he said, turning his dark chocolate eyes back to her.

Madison felt she understood the term 'butterflies in your stomach' for the first time in her life. "You are doing quite well on my account," Madison breathed. They stared at each other in heavy silence for a minute. Not sure what to do next, Madison reached around him. "I should put these in a vase of water," she said, leaning towards the table beside Henry to reach a small decorative vase that sat there.

Her arm brushed against his chest, and she could feel the heat of his body against hers as she tried to reach the vase. She paused, her face inches from his. Madison found herself staring at his lips. Every part of him is perfect, she thought to herself. What would it feel like to kiss him?

Henry knew her intentions were completely innocent, but he was overwhelmed to find himself suddenly so close to her. He could feel her body moving as she breathed in and out. He was dangerously close to throwing caution and decorum to the wind and kissing her pretty lips. The thrill of attraction raced through both of them.

"Baron Sommerfield is in his study waiting for you," Anne said as she sailed back through the doors into the sitting room. Madison and Henry sprang apart. Madison's eyes widened with dismay, but her mother seemed not to have noticed anything. She darted a glance at Henry but he was looking down, straightening his waistcoat.

"Thank you, Lady Sommerfield," Henry said, standing. He turned back to Madison. "I hope I will see you again soon, Miss Hutton," he promised. He seemed to think for a moment, then he reached for her hand. He drew it to his lips and placed a soft kiss on her knuckles. Then he departed with Hux towards her father's study.

Madison stared after him, her entire body tingling. She did not even hear her mother's excited chatter.

Chapter 5

*M*adison and her parents arrived at Lord Warsham's mansion at exactly the appointed time for afternoon tea two days later. As their carriage entered through the gate, it circled a fountain in the center of the large courtyard.

"My goodness," Anne breathed as she craned her neck to get a better view of the imposing residence. It was impressive, even by London standards. While most members of the nobility owned or rented elegant townhouses in London for the Season, this was nothing short of palatial. Separated from the street by the courtyard and a heavy wrought-iron gate, the mansion was more private and therefore even more alluring.

In any other situation, Madison would have rolled her eyes. But for once, her mother was not exaggerating. As she stepped down from the carriage, Madison did her best not to gawk. Imagine the parties that could be hosted here, she found herself thinking. As she looked around the courtyard, she could imagine the pillars twinkling with candles, the huge floral arrangements that could line the walkway. It would be impressive, especially at night, for carriages turning in to see every window of the imposing house alight.

Madison followed her parents inside, where she was surprised to find Henry, rather than a butler or housekeeper, waiting in the grand entry hall. He greeted her parents politely, but his eyes were locked on hers. "Miss Hutton," he took her hand and raised it to his lips, the same way he had last time they were together. Except that the last time they were together, they had not officially been courting yet. Now, every movement, every glance, was fraught with meaning. Madison felt her heart somersault in her chest.

"Lord Warsham, your home is quite impressive," Madison said frankly, trying to distract herself from her raging emotions.

Henry chuckled. "It does tend to have an impact on people," he agreed.

"Do you entertain much?" Madison asked, looking up at the vaulted ceilings and openly admiring the masterpiece-adorned walls.

"Not as a bachelor." Henry's smile deepened. "But I expect once I am married that will change."

Madison blushed deeply. She was relieved when Henry released her hand and turned back to her parents. "Please come with me. I've had our tea prepared in the rear atrium. It overlooks the gardens."

"Thank you, Lord Warsham," Anne said, accepting his proffered arm. He led them through the entry hall towards the back of the house. There were large arched windows that opened onto the greenspace behind the mansion. In the distance, Madison could see a horse being walked along the hedgerow.

"Do you keep a stable on the grounds, my lord?" Madison asked. It was unusual; most residences in the city did not have room for the accommodation and lodged their horses in stables off the main premises.

"I do," Henry said, pausing so Madison could come alongside him. "My great grandfather purchased the grounds and built the house. He was an avid horseman and specifically looked for a space large enough to accommodate a stable. The stables themselves are not large, but they are sufficient for my needs," Henry explained.

"I have heard that you are an accomplished equestrian yourself, my lord," Anne said, happy for an opportunity to get in a compliment. A handsome, rich marquess was just about the best catch she could have hoped to find for her daughter. And Anne was going to do everything in her power to keep her willful and outspoken daughter from spoiling her chances.

"I enjoy riding immensely," Henry said modestly, though a smile of pride did creep onto his face. Madison noted that. He did consider himself an expert horseman, though he tried to brush off the compliment. *Unfortunately, that would not be a shared interest,* she thought to herself.

Henry led them into a parlor at the back of the house, situated with a view of the manicured gardens and the occasional equine occupant. Anne and Harold took spots in the matched wingback chairs, while Madison seated herself on the edge of the sofa adjacent to her parents. Henry sat down beside her, maintaining a careful and proper distance. But

Madison was acutely aware of the closeness of his body. Less than a foot separated them. As he leaned forward to reach for a biscuit, his knee touched hers and it was like a bolt of lightning running through her.

"Your home here in London is very lovely," Anne said, sipping her tea primly. "I know that Madison misses the country so. Being here must be a balm to her." She looked pointedly at her daughter over the rim of her teacup.

Madison was going to roll her eyes, but a sharp glance from her father kept her in check. Instead, she looked away from her mother and turned towards Henry instead. "I do love Sommerfield. I have always felt very at home out-of-doors. Perhaps you would show me the grounds here sometime ….?" She trailed off.

Before Henry could respond, Anne burst in. "Yes, Madison is a good rider herself. I am sure she would love to see your highly praised stables."

Madison snorted aloud. Her mother's eyes rounded like saucers in embarrassment. But Madison just laughed: "You must be confusing me with your other daughter, Mother. I will ride if I absolutely must, but altogether a carriage is the place for me."

Anne looked painfully awkward, but Henry came to the rescue, charming as ever. "Miss Hutton, it would be my pleasure to show you some of the grounds now, if your parents would permit it?"

Harold looked dubious about sending his daughter out of his sight, but Anne nearly fell over herself in her hurry to acquiesce. "Of course, of course! We will enjoy the view from this lovely lookout!"

Henry offered his arm and Madison took it gratefully. She waited until they were out of earshot of her parents before breathing an audible sigh of relief. "Thank goodness you took the hint!" She said with a genuine smile.

Henry laughed as he led her past the arched windows and outside into the early afternoon sunlight. "I don't know if your father was too keen, but I am happy to oblige."

Madison waved her hand dismissively. "My mother will bring him around. He does everything she wants."

"That is an interesting relationship," Henry observed.

"My mother is an interesting woman," Madison said sarcastically. But then her smile softened. "Believe it or not, they really are perfect together. My father is calm and steady, the complete counterpart to my mother's drama. What are your parents like?" She asked.

"My parents passed away some time ago," Henry said. Madison instantly felt a rock drop into the pit of her stomach, but Henry's cheery façade did not falter.

"I am sorry, I did not think," Madison said frowning. "Of course, since you are the Marquess, your father must have already passed on. I should have realized –"

Henry shook his head and laid his hand on her arm reassuringly. "It is quite alright, Miss Hutton. My parents died in a carriage accident when I was quite young. I have come to terms with it completely."

"How young were you when they passed?" Madison asked gently, despite Henry's protestations that he was impervious to related distress.

"I was thirteen. My sisters were all married already, so I was the only one at home."

"That must have been very difficult for you. My mother drives me to distraction sometimes, but I also cannot imagine growing up without her," she said sympathetically.

Henry smiled slightly. "I can see how your mother might have that effect," he said. Madison bit her lip to stop the little laugh that elicited. "It was difficult, I do not deny that. But I was the last child; my eldest sister is almost twenty years my senior. My father started training me to run the marquessate as soon as I could walk, read, and write. I sometimes think that he worried he was short on time to teach me everything he needed, having had me so late in life," Henry explained. His charming little smile stayed in place, no sadness showing on his face.

"You were the much-awaited son?" Madison asked, filling in the blanks of her knowledge of him. He had the easy-going confidence of a youngest child, one who had frequently been doted on. But as far as she could tell, none of the often-associated spoiled, self-centered nature.

"Indeed, I was," Henry grinned.

"Your parents must have been thrilled."

"No one wanted the title to pass to my cousin Toddy. He is a nice enough fellow, but known for being a little too deep in his cups."

Madison smiled. It was interesting that he kept the conversation so light-hearted, even when discussing something as saddening as his parents' death. She wanted to pry deeper but his smile was infectious as they strolled in the spring sunshine. She decided to leave it there for now.

"Thank you for telling me," Madison said genuinely.

"Your concern is endearing, Miss Hutton," Henry answered, continuing to lead her along the paved pathways of the gardens.

Madison nodded, looking away. She gazed around her, admiring the pristinely maintained gardens and trying to think of what to say. "I really would like it if you would call me Madison," she finally said, deciding to completely change the topic.

Henry's eyebrows shot up. "I do not think your mother or father would find that very appropriate," he said, but his eyes glimmered. He was amused rather than disapproving.

"Well, perhaps around them we should stick to Miss Hutton. But when it is just the two of us ... I really am just Madison."

"You are not 'just' anything," Henry said, his smile deepening. "I should not be surprised to find you so unconventional. I knew the minute you crossed a ballroom to introduce yourself that I was not dealing with a typical *ton* debutante."

"I hope never to be characterized as a typical *ton* debutante," Madison said honestly.

"No one would mistake you for typical," Henry said, unconsciously slowing to a stop as he looked down into her eyes. She had such arresting eyes: a unique hazel mixture of gold and green ... like the changing leaves in autumn. And unlike so many young women he knew, including those of his own family, she did not look away when he met them. She stared back at him boldly. "Please, call me Henry," he said.

He was rewarded with a smile that made her even more beautiful. Her smile reached all the way to her brilliant eyes, accentuating a face that was framed by wisps of her bright golden hair.

"Henry," she said, trying the word out. On her tongue, it sounded like music. Without thinking, he reached out and touched the side of her face, his fingertips grazing the side of her cheek. He felt her sharp intake of breath; no one had ever touched her like this before, he was certain. "Henry," she whispered again, this time her voice raspy and unsure.

He was going to lean down and kiss her. He was already imagining how her soft, full lips would feel pressed against his. But then he drew back suddenly. She was not some random *ton* connection or wealthy widow. This was the young woman he was actively courting, whose parents were surely watching closely through the wide windows of the atrium only a hundred yards away. Henry managed to regain control of himself. But he could not wipe the huge grin off of his face.

"Perhaps we should return you to your parents, Madison, before we give them too much cause to worry," he said with a wink. It disguised the desire raging inside him.

Madison was flushed with heat from some new and unknown source. "If you say so … Henry." The familiarity brought a smile to her face, and as they walked inside arm-in-arm, they were to all observers the perfect picture of a young, enraptured couple.

Chapter 6

*M*adison was quickly coming to love the fast-paced glamour of London. She enjoyed hearing the sounds of the streets coming alive when she rose in the morning. She reveled in the availability of a wide range of news sheets; she had never been so well-apprised of current events. In the country, news was always a few days and often a few weeks old. And of course, she relished the never-ending parties and opportunities to socialize that the London season provided.

There was something to do every single night; multiple things to do. Although their family dwelled primarily in the country, it seemed that Madison's mother had spent the last two decades preparing for the day she would launch her daughter onto society. Anne maintained correspondence with half of the ton's ladies. From the moment they had arrived in London, the Hutton family had been flooded with invitations from Anne's carefully curated social network. Madison's promising debut had only increased the wave of envelopes arriving daily.

"Which do you think Lord Warsham is likely to attend?" Anne asked, handing three gilded invitations to Madison.

"How should I know?" Madison scoffed, opening the first envelope. It was to an art exhibition.

"You have spoken privately on multiple occasions." Anne pointed out.

"Three, Mother. We have spoken privately on three occasions. I do not think that makes me an expert on Lord Warsham's choice of *ton* activities." Setting aside the first invitation, Madison opened the second. This one was a singing concert being given by another debutante who had been presented at court alongside Madison. "Though I can tell you, he won't be at that one. I do not think I want to go myself." She tossed the invitation on the table between them.

Anne tried not to smile. While she might agree with her daughter, she would never say something so uncouth. "Don't you want to see him again?" She asked instead.

"Of course I do. But sifting through our invitations to discern where we might be able to ambush him seems a bit much." Just the thought of seeing Henry again made Madison's heart beat more rapidly.

"I do not appreciate your word choice."

"What words would you prefer I use?"

Anne sighed in exasperation. "It is not an ambush. You are courting. Formally."

"Does that mean I cannot also be courted by other men?"

Her mother looked like she'd been hit over the head. "Have you lost your mind? He's a *marquess.*"

"Oh Mother, I was jesting." Madison rolled her eyes and opened the third invitation her mother had handed her. It was for a ball. Madison scanned the details before handing it directly to her mother.

"A ball?" Her mother frowned, looking at the paper. "What makes you he would attend this over any of the others?"

"Honestly, I do not think it likely that he will attend any of them," Madison said. Her mother shot her an annoyed look, so she continued: "He is a bachelor. He probably spends a lot of time at his gentleman's club. That invitation mentions that there will be gaming tables set up. It seems the most likely of the three to draw a young, unmarried man's attention."

"Very clever," Anne said softly, rereading the invitation. She nodded her head with satisfaction. "Thank you, dear. I will send our response now. Be ready to leave on time." With that she pulled out a sheet of paper to pen their reply, turning away and effectively dismissing her daughter.

Madison left the room, muttering under her breath that *she* was not the one in the family known for making a fuss about their appearance. Her mother was gracious enough to ignore her.

The dancing was already underway when Madison arrived with her mother and father. Anne excused herself immediately, determined to investigate whether Lord Warsham was already present or had accepted his invitation for the evening event. Harold took his daughter's arm and led her around the room.

"You're looking for him too," he said quietly after watching Madison for a few minutes.

Madison almost denied it, but then gave a sheepish smile instead. "Am I that obvious?"

"You are not as obvious as your mother, I will give you that," he said with a chuckle. "But your head has been on a swivel since we walked in the door."

"I suppose I am hoping to see Lord Warsham tonight," Madison admitted.

"Didn't you receive a note from him this afternoon?"

"Yes," Madison nodded. "He's invited me to go for a ride in Hyde Park tomorrow."

"Ah," Harold said with understanding. "Your mother must be very pleased with that."

"Yes, she said it was quite important. But I do not understand what is so significant; it is just a carriage ride in the park." As she spoke, Madison continued to look over the guests. Her father obliged her, leading her around the perimeter of the ballroom slowly.

"I cannot pretend to know much about the ins and outs of London society," Harold gave a self-deprecating chuckle. "But in my day, promenading through Hyde Park was very *de rigueur* for young couples.

"If you say so," Madison answered absently. Henry was not in the ballroom.

"I am going to the card room. Would you like to walk with me?" Her father asked, inclining his head towards the doorway. "Your young gentleman might be there."

Madison blushed at how easily her father was reading her. "Alright," she nodded.

They passed through a large foyer that connected the ballroom to the library, which this evening had been outfitted with a dozen card tables. Men and women were seated, playing a variety of different games. At this point in the evening the games were mostly lighthearted, an opportunity for people to gossip while they won and lost paltry sums. The real wagering would not start until much later in the evening when the ladies had retreated or retired and only the serious gamblers remained.

Seated at the far end of the room, at a table with four other players and one empty seat, was Henry. Madison froze, her breath catching in her throat.

"Don't get nervous now, my dear," her father said with a smirk. He put his hand on her arm to keep her at his side, and then led her through the collection of tables towards Henry.

"I do not think the Commons realizes the depth of public animosity towards the income tax," Henry said to Lord Grower, seated on his left.

"The Commons may purport to represent the people, but that does not mean they are truly interested in hearing what they have to say," Lord Grower said passively as the next hand was dealt.

"But do you think –" Henry broke off, coming to his feet quickly and almost upsetting the card table. "Miss Hutton!"

"Good evening, Lord Warsham," Madison said, a smile growing on her face. The other men at the table stood halfway up, making the quick requisite bow before resuming their seats. But Henry continued standing.

"Deal me out of this hand," he said, stepping away from the table. Madison's father led her around the table, lifting her hand from his arm and offering it to Henry. Henry took it instantly, raising her gloved fingers to his lips. He imagined he could feel the warmth of her skin through the silk gloves. "I did not expect to see you this evening."

"Nor did I expect to find you here," Madison said. She hoped he could not feel the way her hand, *nay, her whole body*, seemed to be trembling. "I did not think a ball to be your type of evening entertainment."

"Isn't a ball a proper place to find a marquess?" He teased.

"Oh yes, I would think so. I just did not think you a typical marquess."

Henry laughed as she echoed back the words he had used just days previously. He realized he was still holding her hand. "You are right, Miss Hutton. As a rule, I do not spend much time socializing with the *ton* writ large. But one does have to put in a few appearances, for propriety's sake. And there are card tables on offer this evening." He motioned toward the open seat, leaning around her to speak to her father. "Baron Sommerfield, would you like to join us? We have an open seat."

"Thank you for the invitation, my boy. But I see an old friend just there," Harold pointed to a table occupied by much older gentlemen in the other corner of the room. "I think I will leave you young people to enjoy yourselves."

"Fair enough. Good luck to you, sir," Henry said politely. Madison waved at her father as he departed, leaving her alone with Henry but also completely surrounded by people.

"Would you like to dance? I can leave the game," Henry offered, nodding back towards the ballroom from whence Madison and her father had come.

"No, no, of course not. You are enjoying yourself here. I am just happy to have seen you," Madison said honestly. Henry was still holding her hand. She was hyperaware of every place where his fingers touched hers, even with the layer of her silk gloves between them. His strong index finger held the underside of her fingers, his knuckles pressed against her palm. His thumb held her fingertips, and every few seconds he stroked his thumb casually across the tops of her fingers. It was so intimate and yet so innocent that no one else in the room noticed or cared.

Henry wanted to touch her more. He longed to pull her hand against his chest and run his other hand up the bare skin between the top of her evening glove and the cap sleeve on her shoulder. He thought if he did, she would shiver. He had seen the little tremor run through her body once before, and he wanted to do it again. To watch her bite her lip as she felt the feeling, innocent but sensual. He was not particularly interested in dancing, but he also did not want to let her go.

"Perhaps you would stay and be my good luck charm?" He suggested.

"Of course," Madison agreed without a second thought. As much as she hated to admit it to herself, her mother had been correct. She wanted to see him and spend more time with him whatever the setting or circumstance. They were courting. He could be the love match she had always dreamed about.

While they had been talking, another gentleman had come and filled the seat next to Henry. At his shoulder stood a young woman, perhaps five or six years older than Madison, who was also watching the game unfolding. Henry resumed his seat. Madison decided to mirror the other young woman, moving to stand behind Henry's right shoulder.

Madison knew enough about the card game to follow along as the hands were dealt and the players considered their cards. But she was much more interested in Henry. The other couple must be married, Madison thought to herself. The lady was not just standing behind the gentleman; her hand was resting familiarly on his shoulder, and every few minutes she would lean forward and whisper something in his ear.

In front of her, Madison watched Henry with fascination. She studied the way his shoulders rose and fell as he breathed in and out. She was able to see every strand of gold woven into his otherwise brown hair, giving it that unique sparkle when it hit the light. She wanted to reach out and touch him, the way the other woman touched the man seated before her. Of course, Madison knew that would be completely improper. But without realizing it, she drifted forward so that her gown was pressed up against the back of his chair.

Henry was so aware of Madison standing behind him that he was struggling to focus on the cards in his hand. He was usually a very adept card player, but he had lost three hands in a row. She was standing right behind him. He could sense her closeness, like a bowstring the moment before it was played. He yearned to touch her. Swallowing hard, he resituated himself in his chair and in doing so slid his arm back so it skimmed her leg through the many folds of her dress. The touch was so light it could have been an accident; he was sure she must have thought so, if she noticed it at all. As he leaned back in his chair he realized that her hand was gripping the top of it. His shoulder rested innocently against her fingers. He expected her to pull back her hand. But she did not.

As the next hand was dealt out, Madison leaned down and said quietly: "I do not seem to be helping your luck."

Henry turned his face up to look at her. "I am lucky just to have you standing here with me," he said smoothly.

"If only that translated to your card play."

"I promise you that I am usually a better player than this."

"I believe you," Madison said sweetly. Inside her chest, her heart was hammering. She would happily stand here with her fingers pressed against his shoulder for the rest of the night.

"It seems I have a reputation to rehabilitate," Henry said with a laugh. He turned back to the table, still intensely aware of the beautiful woman standing behind him.

After several hands, the other young woman drifted towards Madison and introduced herself. As Madison had mused, her husband was the man seated beside Henry. Lady Emily Drake turned out to be a full decade older than Madison, with two young children at home. She and Madison chatted amiably while watching the card game unfolding in front of them.

"You are here with Lord Warsham?" Emily asked when the two women went together to fetch fresh beverages from the refreshment table along the wall.

"I am not here *with* him, exactly. My parents escorted me to the ball. But we are courting, yes." Madison explained.

"Courting?" Emily looked surprised, though she tried to cover it with a quick smile.

An uneasy feeling formed in Madison's stomach. "Do you know Lord Warsham?"

"Not well," Emily shook her head. "Only by reputation."

"He assures me his performance this evening is not indicative of his reputation for cards," Madison said, trying to keep the conversation lighthearted as they drifted back towards the card table.

Emily obliged her with a little laugh. "It's not, I assure you. Lord Warsham is well known for his prowess at cards. That was not what I meant, though. He ..." The woman paused, as if unsure whether to continue.

"Please," Madison urged her, though she was not sure she wanted to hear what the other woman had to say.

"I do not know you well, Miss Hutton, and I do not mean to intrude on your private business ..." Lady Drake began, looking uncomfortable. Madison offered her an encouraging smile, which seemed to help her continue. "He has a reputation as a skirt-chaser, a bit of a rogue if you know what I mean?"

Madison's face must have shown her distress because Emily hurried on: "I have never heard of him jilting a woman, or taking advantage. Nothing like that. He is just ... his name has been associated with *a lot* of women."

The uneasy feeling in Madison's stomach coalesced into real worry. A rogue was *not* what she wanted. A rogue was completely antithetical to what she was searching for: a love match.

Emily Drake watched Madison's face. "I shouldn't have said anything," she said worriedly.

Madison reached over and squeezed her hand, giving her a brave smile. "Thank you, I appreciate it. I am just getting to know Lord Warsham. I am sure as we continue our acquaintance, his true nature will be revealed."

Thankfully, the words sounded more confident than Madison felt. They returned to the table, resuming their places standing behind their respective gentlemen's shoulders. Lady Drake mostly stayed by her husband, occasionally casting an apologetic look Madison's way.

Standing behind Henry, Madison tried very hard not to let this new bit of information get to her. She did not want a rogue or a rake. She wanted a loving, committed marriage. What category did Henry truly fall in, she wondered? Every interaction they'd shared indicated his genuine interest.

As much as Madison tried to push the worry aside, it persistently niggled at her. Tomorrow Henry was going to take her for a ride through the park. It would be just the two of them and she would have an opportunity to ask her questions. And make sure she received satisfactory answers.

When Henry fetched Madison from her home the next day, he was nearly bursting with anticipation. It had been the sweetest kind of torture, to have her hovering at his shoulder all night, talking to him in hushed tones, but not ever being able to touch her or actually have a private moment. An open carriage ride through Hyde Park was hardly a private event. It was an outing designed to do just the opposite: announce to the *haute ton* that the Marquess of Clydon and Miss Madison Hutton, daughter of Baron Sommerfield, were officially courting.

But because they were in his phaeton, in the open air for the whole of London society to see, they did not require a chaperone. So, for once, they could converse at their leisure without Madison's mother swooping in to ensure all propriety was observed.

Madison had originally scoffed at her mother for the importance she put on the outing, but once she was riding through the park with Henry at her side she had to admit that her mother was correct. It was a place to see and be seen. And it seemed like half of London's elite were in the park that day, watching them as they drove along the lanes and fields.

She was unusually quiet, Henry noticed right away. She said all the expected pleasantries and kept a smile fixed on her face, but he could tell she was distracted. Attempting to draw her into conversation, he nudged her arm and nodded towards a knot of people gathered along the bank of the Serpentine. Madison followed his eyes.

"See that gentleman there, in the red waistcoat?"

Madison followed his gaze, "Yes?" She said, looking at him questioningly.

"Last night after you left, I took him for almost two hundred pounds."

Madison's mouth dropped open. "You're jesting!"

"Not at all."

"Two hundred pounds?" She repeated, aghast.

"Indeed," Henry said with a grin.

"That is a small fortune!"

"Some people lose them habitually."

"Are you one of those people?"

"Not usually," Henry said with complete honesty.

Madison stared at the young man in wonderment. He was standing with several other gentlemen playing a ball-tossing game in the grass at the water's edge. In his bright red waistcoat, he stood out as the young dandy that he was. "He appears unworried to have lost such a handsome sum."

"His father is a duke," Henry said. "And not one who is hurting for income."

"Do you play games with those kinds of stakes regularly?" Madison asked, turning back to Henry.

"No," Henry shook his head with a small laugh. "I enjoy a gamble, but I also have an estate to protect. Two hundred pounds here and there will not break the marquessate; but if one makes a habit of it, things can go sideways quickly."

Madison nodded. "I've heard about such things, of course. About young lords who gamble away the family money."

"It's not always just the young lords, unfortunately," Henry added. It was not a conversation he would have envisioned having with a proper young woman whom he was courting, but Madison was not ordinary. And it had gotten her talking. Her posture had relaxed, and now her leg was lightly pressed against his as they jostled along in the phaeton.

"Speaking of young lords …" Madison said hesitantly. She did not want to make things uncomfortable, but her mind had been buzzing nonstop since the evening before. If Henry was not the man she thought, if he was a rake, she needed to know.

"Yes?" Henry asked obligingly, shifting his eyes forward as he expertly guided the horses that drew the open carriage along a curve in the path.

"What has your experience been like here in London ... as a young lord?" She asked.

Henry felt his eyebrows raise, though he was not sure if Madison noticed from where she sat next to him. He was not exactly sure what she was asking him, though he had his suspicions. He glanced over at her. Her lips were pouted out, pink and full. Ripe to be kissed.

"I have enjoyed living in London since I came of age. Before that, I remained mostly in the country at Carcliffe Castle, even after my parents' death."

Taking a deep breath through her pursed lips, Madison spoke again. "I know you like to play cards and to ride. What other entertainments do you use to pass the time, while you are here?"

Henry knew where this was going. "I am involved in parliamentary business a lot of the time. I enjoy going out to watch the horse races at Newmarket now and again. As you have surmised, I am not much for society balls and soirees, but I do attend enough to stay in the good graces of the societal matrons." He knew this was not the answer she was looking for; she wanted to know about his personal history. His romantic history. It was both an understandable and wildly inappropriate question for a young woman, and therefore he should not have been surprised that Madison was asking it.

They bounced over a particularly rough patch of the path, and their bodies were jostled together. Their legs were pressed against each other from hip to knee. Henry could feel the exact length of her leg through her gown. He wanted to drop the rein and place his hand on her knee. Kiss those pert, plush lips of hers. Hell, no wonder she was asking this question. Maybe he was not as good at concealing his desire for her as he thought.

Madison did not know if Henry was purposefully evading her question, or if she was just being unclear. Well, there was nothing else for it. Gritting her teeth, she asked: "And in your time in London, have you become acquainted with many women?"

Henry breathed out, an awkward little laugh escaping his lips. *Damn*, she really was one of a kind.

"I'm sorry," Madison said, sighing. "Lady Drake made a comment last night, and I just ... couldn't let it go."

Henry glanced over at her. She may have apologized, but she was still looking at him expectantly, awaiting an answer. "It's alright, Madison. You've a right to ask if anyone does," he said honestly. "Yes, I have known many women during my time living in London and traveling abroad."

Henry watched Madison's face, seeing the shadow that crossed it. "I see," was all she said.

"I have never been involved with a debutante," Henry said. They were coming to a long, straight stretch of path. He relaxed his hold on the reins, transferring them to one hand. With his other hand, he reached across Madison's lap and caught her hands, which were gripped together tightly.

Despite the roiling in her stomach, Madison let him take her hand. Instead of raising it to his lips or gripping it lightly, he laced their fingers together. It felt so intimate, a little shiver went through her. She was suddenly very aware of how closely they were sitting. Despite her worries she felt her heart leaping as she turned her face up to Henry's.

"I do not want to lie to you, Madison. I have sown my wild oats, so to speak. But I was a younger man, not interested in the future. It is not what I am looking for now," he said, trying to infuse the words with as much genuine feeling as he could. It had never occurred to him that she would be put off by his past; it was a privilege of being a handsome, wealthy marquess. Especially one without a father to rein him in or a mother to guilt him into settling down. But Madison looked thoroughly disconcerted.

"Thank you for being honest," Madison said quietly. She looked down at their hands, resting on his knee. Part of her was screaming: go home, break it off, be done, this is not what you want. The other part, the visceral, romantic part, was speaking just as loudly.

"I am looking for a wife," Henry said simply. It seemed a very forward thing to say; they had only known each other for a couple of weeks. They were courting, and of course, he had expressed his interest genuinely to her father. But this declaration felt just short of an actual proposal.

He tugged on the reins and the horses came to a stop. He hooked them over his knee so his other hand was free. Then he used that hand to hook a finger under Madison's chin and lift her eyes to his. The golden-green hazel orbs shone in the afternoon sunlight, her light brown eyebrows piqued as she met his eyes. "I am looking for a wife," he repeated, this time more quietly.

"And I am looking for a husband," Madison said softly, totally transfixed in his warm brown-eyed gaze.

It pained him to say it but he forced the next words out, his eyes never wavering from hers: "Should I take you home?"

Madison felt herself shaking her head. Slowly at first and then more definitively. She watched his perfect mouth curve into a smile and felt her own lips moving to mirror his.

"Ho there!" A voice called, interrupting their reverie. They both turned towards the voice, coming from a rider several yards away down the path. Madison straightened, pulling her hands back into her lap and folding them neatly. Henry picked up the reins automatically, in case the horses spooked at the other rider's approach.

"Theodore!" Henry waved to the other man, recognizing him as he came closer. Madison's ears perked up; Henry had mentioned Theodore Alston before. He was a close friend, the first of Henry's inner circle that she would have met.

"Good afternoon, Henry," Theodore nodded as he came adjacent to them and tugged on the reins to keep his horse in place.

Henry spoke up: "Theodore, please allow me to introduce Miss Madison Hutton, daughter of Baron Sommerfield." He then nodded back towards his friend. "Miss Hutton, this is Theodore Alston, Earl of Willingham. Theodore and I have known each other since we were teenagers when we attended Harrow together."

"I remember," Madison said, smiling at Theodore as she took him in. Even mounted on horseback, Madison could tell that he was tall. Though not as tall as Henry. He had dark hair and was dressed conservatively in sober, muted gray and black. "I am so pleased to meet you, Lord Alston. Lord Warsham has spoken of you several times. He is most lucky to have a friend like you here in London, with all of his family so far afield."

"I suppose so," Theodore said. He glanced at Henry, who raised his eyebrows.

"I have not seen you at any of *ton* gatherings so far this Season. Do you abhor the social whirl as much as Lord Warsham?" Madison asked.

"More so," Theo answered.

"What a pair you two make," Madison said, her voice laced with amused sarcasm. Theodore raised his eyebrows now. Henry tried not to laugh.

"Do not be too hard on him, Ma—Miss Hutton," Henry said, just stopping himself from using her given name. Theodore looked between the two, wondering just what his friend had gotten himself into. Madison looked pleased. Henry decided to stop torturing his friend. "If you will excuse us, Theo, I should return Miss Hutton to her parents before they think something is amiss."

"Of course. Have a pleasant afternoon, Miss Hutton." Theodore bowed his head respectfully.

"I expect we shall talk more soon," Madison said with a cheeky smile. Neither Henry nor Theo was sure if that was a promise or a threat. But the latter departed before she could entrap him further.

"I think you scared him a little bit," Henry chortled as he urged the horses forward and the phaeton lurched into motion once more.

"He is your dearest friend. I expect we will get to know one another better as time goes on." Madison turned to look over her shoulder, watching Theo's horse disappearing solitarily in the opposite direction. "He is a rather lonely fellow, isn't he?" She mused.

"What makes you think so?"

"Just a feeling, I suppose. Perhaps I could introduce him to —"

"I will stop you right there. Theodore has no interest in courting or marriage."

Madison could tell there was more to that story, but she did not press it. "Fair enough," she said, turning back around in her seat. She pushed Theodore Alston to the back of her mind. It was not hard to do; as they wove their way out of the park, Henry took her hand in his again, capturing both her attention and her heart.

Chapter 7

A week later, Madison was still struggling to understand the feelings that Henry had awoken in her. Sitting side by side with him as they had ridden through Hyde Park, their legs pressed together with every jolt of the wheels, had been … well, frustrating, to say the least. She knew she was yearning for … something. But she could not put her finger on what exactly it was she wanted.

As she sat in their family carriage adjacent to her parents, Madison watched her mother and father closely. They were on their way to a musical soiree being given by the Earl and Countess of Spencer. Anne and Harold were talking quietly, absorbed in their conversation and largely ignoring Madison. At the moment, they were specifically discussing a letter her father had received from the steward back at Sommerfield regarding the collection of this quarter's rents. Madison had heard them have such conversations a thousand times; they valued one another's opinions. But that was not what she was watching for. She was trying to detect any sense of the fire that she felt raging inside of her every time she was with Henry.

Her father's hand rested on her mother's knee. They were sitting close together, but there were none of the heated glances or blushes that she was constantly falling victim to when Henry looked her way. She watched them carefully for the duration of the trip but gleaned nothing. She was shaking her head by the time they arrived at the seasonal home of the Earl and Countess of Spencer. Madison was deep in her own mind as she climbed down from the carriage; so much so that she did not realize the person who handed her down.

"Henry!" She cried, shocked to find herself hand-in-hand with him all of the sudden.

Madison's mother looked scandalized. She opened her mouth to correct her daughter's very inappropriate use of the Marquess' given name, but Henry broke in before she could speak.

"Good evening, Baron Sommerfield, Lady Sommerfield," he bowed politely and raised Madison's hand to his lips as had become his custom when greeting her. "Miss Hutton," he said, smiling over her hand.

"Your timing is impeccable, *Lord Warsham*," Madison said, heavily emphasizing the address. Henry looked like he might burst out laughing, but instead he took her hand firmly in his and started to lead her inside. Madison leaned over and said quietly: "Do you have to be so perfect all of the time? My mother already thinks I am a heathen."

Henry did not break stride or laugh at all, but he was struggling to keep it in. "I will endeavor to be less perfect … *Madison*."

Madison glanced over her shoulder at her mother, who was watching them with sharp eyes. She shrugged. "It is a lost cause." This time Henry did laugh, and rather than look back to see her mother's approval or lack thereof, Madison instead let herself bathe in the warm sound.

As they entered the crowded townhouse, she felt many eyes shift towards them. This was only the second time they had appeared together in public, but Madison knew they were causing quite a stir. The attention being paid to one specific young woman by a highly eligible marquess was the kind of gossip London's *haute ton* thrived on. But Madison did not mind all the eyes being on her; not when she was so blissfully happy. She looked up at Henry towering tall above her and her body flooded with warmth. He was charming, funny, and kind. He was already an ally when it came to her exasperating mother.

She was reflecting on how worried she had been that first night at Lady Herrin's ball and feeling thankful she had not hesitated to approach Henry herself, when a familiar face emerged from the crowded room to their left.

"Madison!" Eve waved. Extracting her arm from her husband's, she gave Madison a boisterous hug. "You look more beautiful every time I see you, darling," Eve said, but she was already turning her eyes to Henry. She elbowed her friend discreetly.

"Eve, this is Henry Warsham, Marquess of Clydon. Lord Warsham, may I present my friend and her husband, Lord and Lady Brockton." Madison executed the introductions, watching her friend's reactions. She had not had the chance to discuss her courtship with Henry with anyone other than her parents, and she was dying for a moment alone with Eve.

Her friend seemed to agree. "David, darling, would you and Lord Warsham fetch Madison and I some refreshments? From what I have heard, the French musical trio that Countess Spencer hired for this soiree is quite good, and I do not want to miss anything once they start playing," Eve said smoothly.

Henry looked at Madison to see her response. She nodded subtly, a slight smile gracing her lips. He quirked an eyebrow, murmured something nondescript, and then disappeared with Eve's husband as she had bid.

Madison turned back to her friend, who had been watching the byplay between Madison and Henry closely. A smile crept over Eve's face. "You are smitten."

Chuckling at her friend's forwardness, Madison did not even try to deny it. "I find Henry … fascinating. He is funny, kind, handsome …" Her voice trailed off, and she gulped audibly.

"Funny and kind? Madison, that man looks like a god."

Madison shook her head, biting her bottom lip as she watched Henry from across the room. He was easy to spot because of his height. He and Eve's husband, David, had been drawn into conversation with several other men on their way to the refreshment tables. "Eve, I need to ask you …"

Eve's eyebrows raised. "Yes?" She asked with interest.

"Your relationship with David … is it normal … I mean …" Madison struggled to find the words.

"Madison, is something wrong?" Her friend asked. She certainly had Eve's attention now.

"No, nothing is wrong. I just … the way it is with Henry, I do not know if it is normal."

"The way what is? You seemed perfectly natural together."

Madison frowned, her brows furrowing as she tried to articulate the new feelings she had been experiencing in the last few weeks. She felt her cheeks begin to burn, but she forced herself to keep speaking. "When he touches me … holds my arm, helps me into the carriage, when we walk together … Lord, I guess it is every time he looks at me or touches me, I get this feeling deep in my chest."

Eve was biting her lip so hard, Madison could see the redness when her friend finally released it. A huge smile spread across Eve's face. She looked like she was trying very hard not to laugh. "Oh, darling. Yes, that is perfectly normal. What you are feeling is attraction, desire, dare I say it … lust."

"What?" Madison was shocked to hear the word from her friend's mouth.

"Don't look so scandalized, Maddie." Eve put a reassuring arm around her. "You *want* to be attracted to the man you intend to marry. Trust me, it makes the whole arrangement more enjoyable."

"You do not often hear the word 'lust' associated favorably with marriage." Madison pointed out skeptically.

Eve waved her hand dismissively. "Trust me on this one, Madison. If these are the feelings you are having for him, then I am sure he is having them for you. This is exactly what you wanted."

"Lust does not equal love. Besides, I know my parents love each other deeply, and I have never seen anything like this between them," Madison countered.

Eve grimaced. "And let us hope that we never have to," she said. "This is not the type of thing you want to see between your parents anyways. But I can assure you, what happens behind closed doors between a couple in love ..." Eve just sighed dreamily and looked across the room at her husband. Madison watched her with interest; her eyes had taken on a slightly glassy look, her breathing was coming a little heavier, and a light blush had bloomed over her cheeks and bosom.

"Will you excuse me, Maddie? I think I will go find my husband," Eve said with a distracted smile.

"Of course. Thank you, Eve." They touched cheeks and then Eve drifted off through the crowd, leaving Madison alone.

"... Miss Hutton ..."

Madison heard her name float through the crowd and turned towards the direction she had heard it: a small group of four women chatting a few feet away. Without thinking, she walked towards them, thinking she was being summoned.

Henry watched Madison from across the room, chatting with her friend Eve. Eve's husband had continued to talk to a group of other young men about their age, but Henry managed to detach himself. He took a glass of punch off the refreshment table and sipped it while he looked at her. He was having a harder and harder time keeping a clear head when he was around her. The more time he spent with her, the more he was taken in.

He had instantly found Madison interesting and unusual. As he got to know her better over the past few weeks, he found her to be clever, friendly, and easy to spend time around. She was equally comfortable in one-on-one conversations and crowded ballrooms with all eyes on her. And the physical yearning she inspired … well, he took another sip of punch.

While he had not expected this level of attraction to his future wife, he was pleased to find it. Fulfilling physical relationships were not a hallmark of most *ton* marriages. Most married couples he had known, his parents included, never showed anything beyond a passing interest in one another. The production of heirs was just another box to be checked off. But Henry had no doubt that with Madison, creating heirs would be nothing less than spectacular.

He watched as Madison embraced her friend Eve in farewell, and then the latter departed. Henry started through the crowd to regain Madison's hand before some other interested gentleman could try to engage her. As he approached, he saw her walk closer to a knot of other young women, and then freeze suddenly.

"… Miss Hutton? Of course, I have noticed. How could I not?"

"It is embarrassing."

"Yes!"

"Who does she think she is? A short little nobody, from a baronage in the middle of nowhere, courting with the Season's most eligible, the Marquess of Clydon? It's laughable!"

Henry watched Madison's face as they both overheard the conversation. She initially looked shocked as she realized she wasn't being invited into the conversation; she *was* the conversation. Then her eyes narrowed. Henry stepped forward, intending to take her away from the situation immediately. Madison spotted him, but she shook her head and instead stepped towards the circle of young women.

"Miss Rippen, Lady Hoth, I thought I heard you calling me!" Madison said brightly, inserting herself in between the two aforementioned ladies. She turned towards the other two women. "I do not believe I have had the pleasure of making your friends' acquaintance," she said, keeping her smile fixed firmly on her face.

"I … Miss Hutton …" Miss Rippen stuttered, looking aghast. Lady Hoth was not so easily embarrassed. She pursed her lips, looking pleased with herself.

"This is Lady Merrywright, and my cousin Miss Quinn." Lady Hoth introduced the two other women, staring down her nose at Madison.

"I hope you are enjoying yourselves this evening. I know the Marquess and I …" Madison glanced over her shoulder as if she had just realized that Henry was standing behind her. "Oh, Henry, there you are!"

Henry stepped forward as he was summoned, sensing what Madison was playing at. He reached down and took her hand, making a show of lingering over it before tucking it into his arm. "Madison," he said her given name like a caress. And even in front of these snobby *ton* women, Madison felt her heart do a little flip-flop. Henry continued smoothly: "I apologize for leaving you alone for so long. I have arranged with Countess Spencer for the two most excellent seats for the performance."

"That sounds lovely." Madison stared up at him adoringly. Though she knew the impact it was making, it was not an act. She could easily have looked up into his handsome face, those warm, twinkling eyes, and forgotten everything else. But they were playing out an act, and she was not going to let the issue drop. She forced a little pouting frown to her face and turned back to the other women. "Oh, please do join us? That would not be too difficult to arrange, would it?" Madison asked Henry.

Henry suppressed a laugh. "Anything for you," he managed to say with a straight face. He started to lead her away and Madison motioned for the other women to follow them.

"That was very well done," he whispered to Madison.

She smiled mischievously. "Having to sit next to us for the entire performance sounds like a fitting punishment."

This time Henry did not even bother stopping his laugh.

Chapter 8

*H*enry sat across from the well-dressed gentleman in the formal parlor, examining offering after offering. He looked closely at the diamonds, rubies, sapphires, and emeralds that the jeweler passed to him. Small and gray-haired, the bespectacled man was giving detailed descriptions of each gem as he presented it to the Marquess of Clydon. But Henry was listening with only half an ear.

As he considered a large emerald in a bright gold setting, he found himself wondering if perhaps something of his mother's might be more appropriate. But that would take time. He would need to contact his sisters, arrange to visit them, or have them come to London. He would have to explain himself to them. While he did not doubt their approval, it would take a few weeks, maybe a month, to arrange and execute the whole exchange. *No*, he decided. He did not want to wait.

Madison was the wife for him. After watching her face down those catty women at the Spencer soiree, he was completely certain. Sure, he had planned for them to be seen together in public three times at least, and they had only been out twice. But despite that he could see no reason to wait. He had set out to find a wife, and by some stroke of luck he had met her right away. She would be the perfect marchioness. The next steps would be to propose, have the banns read, and get married.

Feeling very pleased with himself, Henry nodded as he turned the ring over and over between his fingers. "Yes, this will do."

"An exquisite selection, my lord!" The jeweler assured him. "I will have it polished and delivered to you in two days."

Henry shook his head. "I need it today, this evening."

"My lord –"

"I am happy to compensate you for the inconvenience. But I need it tonight." Henry insisted. He was supposed to meet Madison this evening to escort her to a play, with her mother accompanying them as a chaperone.

The other man nodded slowly, noting the determined look in Henry's eyes. "I can have it ready this evening, sir, if you can pick it up?"

"Yes, of course." Henry nodded, but he was once again deep in his thoughts.

"He is here already?" Madison clarified, from where she was sitting on the edge of her mother's bed. The housekeeper nodded.

"That is highly unusual. We are not supposed to leave for half an hour at least." Anne frowned but did not turn her head as a maid worked to dutifully arrange her hair. "He will have to wait, I suppose –"

"I am ready!" Madison said eagerly. "I will go down now."

She was already halfway out the door as her mother called: "Behave yourself! Do not close the door to that sitting room!"

Madison rolled her eyes and continued down the hall. She was dressed in one of the most formal gowns she owned, sea-green silk overlaid with pale gold translucent organza. A line of little turquoise beads was stitched beneath the ruched bust, which displayed a large expanse of her pale skin. She had even donned elbow-length midnight blue silk evening gloves. After a considerable row with her mother about appropriate hairstyles, she was wearing a jeweled broach fashioned into a hair adornment at the nape of her neck, with the rest of her hair cascading down her back.

She caught a glimpse of her reflection in a windowpane as she reached the stairs. She nodded, pleased with what she saw. If her encounter with those vile women had taught her anything, it was that people were going to talk about her even more now that she and Henry were courting so publicly. The gossip did not bother her and neither did the harsh words; she was quite secure in herself and what she had to offer. But she also wanted Henry to be proud of her. If she was going to give people something to talk about, at least let it be on her terms.

Henry was not in the foyer. She found him waiting in the sitting room, standing casually against the mantlepiece. He straightened as soon as he saw her. "Hello," Madison said, smiling when he took her hand and kissed it. She had come to expect this greeting, was even holding out her hand in advance. It warmed her to realize that she was getting to know Henry's habits.

"Hello," Henry echoed. He kissed her knuckles, but then looked over her shoulder questioningly. He did not release her hand. "Are your mother or father going to join us?"

He looked a little bit nervous, Madison thought. She shook her head, watching him carefully. "Not likely. My mother is mid-hairdressing, and my father has learned never to expect my mother to be on time for anything," Madison said. "You, however, are early."

"I wanted to speak with you alone," Henry said. He glanced again over her shoulder towards the doors of the sitting room that opened onto the foyer. There were no servants in sight; it appeared they were alone.

"My mother will kill us if we close those doors," Madison said candidly, following his gaze. She was sure her mother would be downstairs as soon as she could manage it, was perhaps even now deputizing a maid to come and watch over the encounter between them.

"It doesn't matter." Henry shook his head, seeming to shake off whatever discomfort he was feeling. When he looked down at Madison again, he was smiling. "Madison, I have thoroughly enjoyed getting to know you these past few weeks."

"As have I," she said slowly.

"I hope you know that my intentions have been sincere from the beginning," Henry continued. Madison frowned. Henry was one of the most easy-going, comfortable people she had ever met. But he looked decidedly awkward and nervous this evening. Was he about to break off their courtship?

"I never doubted your intentions, Henry. You have been a perfect gentleman," she said. He flushed, a small ripple of laughter rolling through him. While he was still holding her hand, his other was in his pocket quite awkwardly. A split second before he drew it out, Madison realized what was about to happen.

"A perfect gentleman would have been able to wait and court you properly. But I am finding that when it comes to you, my love, I do not have much patience." He pulled the ring out of his pocket.

"Henry …" Madison breathed, her eyes widening like saucers as he held out the spectacular emerald engagement ring. Very deliberately, Henry pulled off her silk glove and laid it aside.

"Madison Hutton, it would be my greatest honor if you would consent to be my wife," Henry said, sliding the ring onto her finger.

Without thinking, Madison found herself in his arms. In her excitement, she had embraced him and he had responded, his arms going around her completely naturally. When their lips met, Madison felt every wave of desire and longing coalesce into a fiery spark between them.

His lips were so soft. How was that possible? Everything about him was masculine and strong. Yet as his lips moved against hers, it was as if they were melting together. He slid his hand around her waist, pulling her closer against him.

She was as warm and intoxicating as Henry had imagined. Without noticing, he had lifted her off the ground so just the tips of her toes touched the earth. He instinctively wanted her closer. Her kiss was innocent but enthusiastic. As he slid his tongue into her mouth, he felt her momentary surprise, and then her welcome as she leaned into him and deepened the embrace.

There was a loud *thump* in the foyer. Madison felt her feet touch the floor, and the instant they did she turned to look behind her. One of the maids had dropped a hatbox she had been carrying on the floor. The poor young woman stood frozen in the foyer. Madison tried to smile reassuringly at the wide-eyed maid. She fought back the impulse to deny that anything untoward had happened; Madison knew well enough that something witnessed by one staff member would soon be known by all.

Trying to look calm and dignified, though her insides were reeling, Madison smoothed her clothes and spoke steadily: "Please ask my mother and father to join us immediately."

The maid nodded, gathered up the hatbox she had dropped on the floor, and scurried up the stairs. When Madison turned back to Henry, he was grinning.

"I will take that as a yes?"

Madison blushed from her hairline to the tips of her toes. "Yes." She nodded emphatically, her radiant smile growing to match his. There was a commotion upstairs, and the sound of hurried footsteps. "Are you ready?" Madison asked, knowing her parents were about to descend upon them.

Henry came to stand beside her. "Ready for anything, love," he said, taking her hand.

Madison felt a flicker of something deep in her stomach. *Love*, Henry called her. But he had not told her that he loved her. As her mother burst into the room, Henry squeezed her hand reassuringly, and Madison did her best to bury the thought.

Chapter 9

The banns had to be read aloud in church three
times before they could be married, so the
wedding date was fixed for one month hence.
Madison's mother was thrilled; she launched into
wedding preparations with the ferocity and
determination of a terrier. Anne told Madison
repeatedly that since her sister, Meera, had deprived
her of a wedding by defecting to Paris, she going to
make sure that Madison's wedding day was perfect.
Perfect by her standards, at least. She was not
particularly interested in soliciting her daughter's
opinions with regards to the planning of the upcoming
nuptials.

Madison kept replaying the scene of Henry's
proposal over and over again in her mind. The kiss …
made her blush. And, if she was being perfectly honest
with herself, it made her yearn for the wedding. She
had a basic understanding of what a wedding night

would entail. But kissing Henry, that was beyond anything she could have ever imagined.

But the words were missing. Madison came to London dead-set on a love match. *Did she love Henry?* She asked herself. Yes, she thought so. She looked forward to spending time with him, she missed him when he was gone, he seemed a true and loyal partner. *Yes, she did love him,* she decided. And while their courtship had been the thing of fairytales, the one thing that was missing was a declaration of love on either side.

She considered speaking with her mother about it, but ultimately Madison decided against it. Madison loved her mother, but she did not think Anne would be able to separate the fact that she had secured a marriage proposal from a marquess from any advice-giving. Madison decided that she would try and talk about it with Eve the next chance that she had. However, the next opportunity she had to speak with Eve was not what she expected at all.

She received a cryptic note from Eve telling her to meet her at the *modiste* at a specified time and to make sure she did not bring her mother. At first, Madison thought it was going to be impossible. Her mother wanted a hand in everything that could be even tangentially related to the wedding. But when Madison described meeting her friend for a fitting, her mother brushed her off and headed in the opposite direction muttering something about floral arrangements.

When Madison arrived at the *modiste*, her friend was waiting outside. Without explanation, Eve looped her arm through Madison's and took her inside.

Madison let Eve lead her across the salon and through a heavily curtained doorway. She looked around curiously; in the many visits she had paid to Madame Janine's boutique with her mother, she had never seen anyone other than the shop girls or the Madame herself go back here. There were no windows, and the decor was ... different. Rich, jewel-toned velvets and heavy satins were draped everywhere. The lighting was low; just a handful of candles placed intentionally here and there, casting long shadows across the mysterious room.

Eve smiled enigmatically as she took a seat on a ruby red chaise and patted the seat next to her. Completely nonplussed, Madison sat down. "What is this room for?"

"This is where the Madame holds fittings of a more ... private nature." Eve's smile deepened when Madame Janine herself entered.

"Lady Brockton, I am so pleased you have returned. But so soon? Was something amiss with your last order?" The tall, older woman curtsied to Eve and Madison and then reached for a nearby table and began filling glasses of wine.

"It was all perfect, as usual. Lord Brockton was most appreciative of your work," Eve assured her, accepting a glass of wine. Madison raised her eyebrows. She had never heard Eve's husband comment on anything as flippant as fashion.

"I am here today with my friend, Madison Hutton. She is to be married soon to the Marquess of Clydon, you see, and I wanted to see about completing her trousseau."

"Eve, you are a dear, but I told you my mother has it completely in hand," Madison interjected. Why were they talking about her trousseau? She had plenty of clothes; her mother had certainly seen to that.

"What I have in mind is not the sort of thing your mother will have taken care of, darling," Eve answered. "Perhaps you can show us some of your more recent designs, so she can get an idea of what she might like?" She directed Madame Janine.

"Of course!" With a quick clap of her hands, Madame disappeared through another doorway.

"I don't understand ..." Madison began. Her mouth fell open in astonishment as several young women followed the Madame out into the dimly lit room.

Each was dressed in a unique confection of lace, silk, and satin. But the dresses – if you could call them that – were unlike anything Madison had ever seen. The first was a robe made of entirely translucent fabric, with artfully applied lace appliques at the breasts and hips. The young woman wore it tied loosely at the waist, so a deep-v of skin reaching almost to her navel was visible. Another wore an intricately stitched bustier which was widely laced across the front so the curves of her breasts were showcased.

"I couldn't possibly wear something like this. In front of Henry? Have you lost your mind?" Madison gaped.

Her friend laughed heartily. "Maddie, I have seen the way you look at that man. And I have seen the way he looks at you. Trust me, you will both enjoy this." She reached across and squeezed Madison's hand, half reassuring, half conspiratorial. "Now, I am partial to the silver."

All thoughts of having a deep, serious conversation with her friend completely fell away from Madison's mind.

Henry was pleased with the way things were progressing. Madison and her mother had the wedding planning entirely in hand. He had seen to the details he needed to, including negotiating the dowry and marriage settlement with Madison's father. It had been a formality, but Henry was pleasantly surprised to hear the assets that Madison was entitled to. Not for his benefit, but because if anything happened to him she would be well provided for with the combination of her bridal endowments and her entitlements from his estate. All in all, it was moving along quite smoothly.

He was planning to take Madison to the opera this evening. Glancing at his pocket watch as he reigned his horse into the courtyard, he judged that he had enough time to work in his office for several hours before he would need to start getting ready.

He was becoming more involved in the arguments around the income tax repeal Madison had heard him discussing with Lord Grower by the day. While he had been slow to get involved in politics when he'd inherited the marquessate as a teenager, after more than a decade in the House of Lords Henry found himself taking a leading role more and more often. The debate about whether or not to repeal the income taxes originally implemented to fund the war with Napoleon was threatening to set England on fire. With the time he had this afternoon, he hoped to pen letters to several prominent leaders in the manufacturing sect with the hope of brokering a meeting with key members of government.

Tucking his pocket watch away, he realized that the courtyard was not empty. A large, stately carriage stood in front of the house between the fountain and the front doors.

While he did not recognize the carriage, he could see that its occupants had been admitted to the house. And very few people could have arrived at his home and been assured of their entrance. Henry gritted his teeth. The correspondence he hoped to accomplish would have to be postponed, hopefully just until later this evening. There was only one question in his mind as he entered the house: which of his sisters was waiting inside?

Henry found them sitting on the back terrace taking tea in the mid-morning sun. "I should have known it was the two of you. You're the only ones nosy enough to show up unannounced." He said wryly from the doorway.

Denise and Erica turned around in unison, though their reactions could not have been more different. Denise was the eldest of the family. At almost twenty years Henry's senior, she had occupied a strange middle-ground of an older sister and surrogate mother for most of Henry's formative years. She looked him over with narrowed eyes and pursed lips.

Erica, conversely, was the youngest of his four elder sisters and the closest in age to Henry. Aged five when her long-awaited younger brother had arrived in the world, they had grown up with a much more traditional sibling relationship. When their parents died, she had been a newlywed. Since then, his interactions with all of his sisters had been intermittent.

Despite that, Erica sprang to her feet and embraced him eagerly. "You're getting married! I am so pleased for you!" She said, a wide smile on her face.

"Nadine and Helen were quite interested in making the trip, but felt that they did not have enough notice," Denise said pointedly. She did stand up and touch cheeks with her brother, but her expression did not change. "I was quite perturbed to hear from *my neighbor* that my little brother was engaged to be married."

Henry grimaced. "I did write to let you all know that I was courting a young woman with an eye towards marriage," he said in his defense.

"Telling us you are thinking about marrying and actually getting married are two different things," Erica admonished, pinching his arm. Henry shook her off. This was exactly why he had not been keeping his sisters apprised of the situation. They had an irritating tendency to treat him like he was still thirteen years old.

"When can we meet her?" Denise asked pointedly, returning to her seat and her cup of tea.

"At the wedding," Henry said jokingly, privately wishing it could be true.

"Nice try," Denise said, raising her cup in mock salute. "How about tonight?"

Henry shook his head: "I am taking Madison to the opera tonight."

"I love the opera!" Erica said excitedly.

"I do not think that is a good idea –"

"I am assuming you still maintain your private box?" Denise asked, a self-satisfied smile spreading over her face. She knew the answer to her question; they had sat in that very same opera box the season before when they were in town for her daughter Louisa's debut.

"Yes," Henry answered, recognizing the trap.

"Then there is plenty of room for us to join you and meet your fiancée." Denise nodded matter-of-factly.

"Don't look so defeated, Henry," Erica said with a sympathetic smile. "You know you cannot hide her from us forever."

"Of course not," Denise said, looking perfectly pleased with her victory. Her light brown hair, once streaked with bright golden highlights like her brother's, was now streaked with gray. But her dark brown eyes were as sharp as ever. "Since mother and father are not here to approve of your choice of bride, it falls to us to make sure you are choosing wisely."

Henry felt a lurch in his stomach at his sister's words. His sisters could not stop him from marrying, he reassured himself. But they could sure as hell make his life more difficult along the way. But Madison was more than up to the task, he reminded himself.

Sighing and accepting defeat, Henry went back inside the house to send a note to Madison directly and let her know about the change of plans.

Madison was pacing in the foyer, waiting for Henry to arrive. She was not a nervous person, she reminded herself over and over again. She was not *normally* a nervous person she amended. But today had totally twisted her into knots.

By the time Madison left Madame Janine's boutique with Eve, her heartbeat had finally slowed down. But she had no idea what she would say to her mother when the packages bearing her newly ordered items arrived at the townhouse. She might die of embarrassment if her mother opened the boxes and saw what was inside. After turning the idea over and over in her head, watching the young women in the boutique moving around sensually, and having her measurements taken, Madison had arrived at the conclusion that Eve was most likely correct. The attraction between her and Henry grew every minute they were together. She could only imagine what his reaction would be to seeing her in one of the negligees she had just ordered.

She arrived home later than she planned, with just enough time to quickly eat something and to dress for the opera. There on her dressing table was a note. Madison had recognized the handwriting immediately; it was from Henry.

After eating a few tea sandwiches, letting her mother select her ensemble, and even allowing her hair to be dressed – mostly because she was too distracted to protest – Madison was now wearing a path across the floor of the townhouse's foyer.

"He is the head of his family," Anne reminded her as she walked in from the back of the house. "His sisters rarely come to London. I cannot imagine they are close."

"They are the only family he has," Madison countered. *What if they did not approve of her?* She would be devastated. Whatever her feelings about love, professed or not, Madison could now envision her happy ending with only one person: Henry.

"Maddie, you are already engaged. The banns have been read. You are going to be married in less than two weeks," Anne reminded her. Her mother was not worried about the hiccup of Henry's older sisters arriving in London unannounced.

What an irritating reversal of fortunes, Madison reflected. Ever since Henry's proposal, Anne had been perfectly serene. Meanwhile, Madison, who had always been so sure of herself, was pacing and questioning. *Enough of this*, she told herself. She was going to be Henry's wife. His sisters would be her sisters. And if there was anything *she* had experience with, it was sisters. She had an elder and a younger and knew the annoyances of each.

"Remember their proper addresses. His eldest sister is a Countess, but the younger one is just an 'Honorable,'" Anne said, her hands resting on her rounded hips.

Madison rolled her eyes. "I plan on calling them by their names, mother. They are going to be my sisters. Could you imagine if I called Leonora 'Lady Avery' every time we were together?"

"It would certainly be more proper," her mother opined.

"And what would I call Meera?" Madison asked.

"A headache," Anne answered definitively. Madison laughed unabashedly, garnering a small, indulgent smile from her mother.

There was a sharp knock, and both women straightened and sobered unconsciously. Madison's mother motioned Hux forward to answer it. Henry appeared in the doorway, looking as handsome as ever. He was wearing a dark gold-colored brocade waistcoat that perfectly pulled the brighter highlights out of his light brown hair. For the first time, Madison found herself wondering what color the hair on his chest would be. Her eyes widened in embarrassment at the thought and a blush flooded her chest and face. She would soon know, she realized. She would see him. All of him.

She gulped audibly. Her mother gave her a strange look as she stepped forward to welcome Henry, looking around curiously for the sisters who he was supposed to have brought with him. "I was most looking forward to meeting your sisters." Madison heard her mother say.

"They are waiting in the carriage. The weather has taken a turn for the wetter, I'm afraid," he said graciously to Anne before turning back to Madison and offering his hand. "Are you brave enough to venture out?" He teased, clearly making light of the inquisition awaiting them outside.

His smile naturally lit Madison's own. "Are you?" She put her hand in Henry's, accepted her cloak from Mrs. Miller, and followed him outside. It was miraculous and marvelous how a smile on his face and her hand in his could give her such a surge of confidence. "You have about ten seconds to give me any warnings before we get in the carriage," she said as they stepped out the door, ignoring the rain.

"Be yourself. They won't stand a chance." Henry winked at her. Madison's heart did a little flip-flop, and the world tipped around her. *No, the world really was tipping around her.* Her toe caught the edge of her dress, she stumbled into a puddle, lost her footing, and landed on her bottom with an ignominious *splat*.

"Madison!" Henry scooped her up quickly, kicking open the door of the carriage and depositing her inside in one flourish. The familiar use of her given name was not lost on his sisters, who exchanged interested glances.

Madison took one look around the carriage, observing the raised eyebrows of the other two women, Henry's dismayed face, noting her sopping wet backside, and let out a self-deprecating laugh. "As you can see, I like to make a splash," she said sardonically.

Henry threw his head back and laughed appreciatively. Erica giggled prettily. Denise shook her head, but there was the barest hint of a smile at the corners of her lips. She spoke first.

"Henry, your gallantry is noted. But perhaps you should help Miss Hutton back inside the house so she can change," Denise said, nodding back towards the townhouse.

Erica nodded in agreement. "Yes, let's get on. I do not want to miss any more of the opera than we must —"

"Oh no," Madison broke in. "We must not delay on my account." She reached up and rapped on the roof of the carriage to signal the driver to go ahead.

"You are soaking wet," Henry protested, tapping the roof of the carriage again himself. The carriage lurched forward, and then stopped again. The poor driver was clearly confused.

"Hardly," Madison argued, but then realized the ridiculousness of that statement. Her cloak had protected her shoulders and the top of her gown. But her backside was wet from landing in the puddle and her hemline was damp for several inches. Her hair was probably askew; the more elaborate the coiffure, the more given to disaster, and her mother had taken full advantage of Madison's distraction this evening. "Perhaps I am a bit disheveled," Madison admitted.

"You look beautiful," Henry said loyally and with complete sincerity. Madison looked up at him, caught by those warm dark eyes. Her hair had come undone in the back so that long tendrils were escaping over her neck and shoulders. When she fell, the hood of her cloak fell back, allowing the rain to fall on her face. Several strands of her golden hair, turned dark by the rain, were stuck to the side of her face. But while most women would have been petrified and embarrassed by such a gaff, Madison looked exhilarated. Her eyes were bright and her delectable breasts were moving up and down as she breathed rapidly.

Denise and Erica exchanged a look as Madison and Henry smiled and sighed and flirted without saying a word. Erica shook her head slightly to discourage her sister from interrupting them, but Denise ignored her. "Ahem." She cleared her throat pointedly.

Madison snapped back to attention. "Please, let's get on. I am sure I can make myself presentable enough. I know you two do not get down to London often, I do not want to deprive you of the treat," Madison said earnestly, addressing Denise and Erica.

Erica's jaw dropped in disbelief. "You cannot be serious…"

"Yes, yes, of course, I am." Gaining confidence, Madison nodded her head and then rapped on the carriage roof again definitively. This time, Henry did not contradict her and the coach started moving forward.

Henry's sisters looked on with surprise and a bit of amusement as Madison sat forward and went to work straightening herself out. She started pulling pins out of her hair. She glanced over at Henry: "Your hand, please?"

He held out his hand obligingly and sat with a growing smile on his face as Madison pulled every single pin out of her hair and deposited each into his hand. Then she ran her fingers through the damp mass, pulling the stray hairs back from her face, twisted it into a knot at the nape of her neck, and took back a few pins from him to secure it in place.

"There," she said with satisfaction, patting her hair gently to check that everything was holding together as it should. "There is not much to do with my dress, I am afraid. But I am not overly bothered. It will dry before the opera is over, I am sure."

Denise watched her brother's fiancée carefully. She knew her mind well enough to admit that she was impressed by Madison's aplomb. She reached up and untied the ribbon that held her own cloak in place.

"Here, take this against the chill," Denise said, pulling the heavy velvet outerwear off of her frame and offering it to Madison.

"I couldn't," Madison protested. "It is still raining. There is no reason for both of us to be wet."

But Denise insisted. "If you can sit through the opera with a soaking wet gown on my behalf, I can certainly handle a few raindrops on my shoulders for yours."

Despite her dampness and the chilly spring evening, Madison felt a warmth start to grow inside of her. "Thank you," she said, accepting the garment.

Henry helped her adjust it over her shoulders as the carriage jolted to a stop in front of the opera house.

Chapter 10

By the time they emerged from the opera house to their waiting carriage several hours later, the rain had finally stopped. Madison chatted amiably with Denise and Erica, while Henry mostly watched in silence from his corner of the carriage. When they arrived outside Madison's parents' townhouse and he handed her down to the doorstep, he was thankful to finally have a moment alone with her.

"Your sisters are lovely," Madison said honestly as they climbed the stairs to the front door.

Henry chuckled. "I am sure they will say the same about you," he assured her.

"Well, I am sure I left a strong impression, at the very least," she said cynically.

"You always do," Henry teased. Madison poked him in the side. They both laughed. He grabbed her hand to prevent her from doing it again. The spark of awareness that went through them as their skin touched stopped their laughter. Madison felt her sharp intake of breath and the flutter of feeling in her chest. "You've made quite an impression on me," Henry said, stroking his thumb over the back of her hand.

Her heart was pounding in her chest. "I do tend to have that effect on people," Madison breathed.

"And here I thought I was special …" he leaned closer; she could feel the warmth of his body nearer to hers.

"You know you are special," Madison tried to tease, but her words were velvety and inviting. Henry did not hesitate. He took the invitation, leaning down to kiss her. His arms went around her, lifting her just slightly off the ground so their lips could meet.

Madison knew a little more what to expect this time, but that did not make kissing Henry any less exhilarating. When his tongue slid into her mouth, she met it with her own. She had thought at first it felt like an invasion. But she realized now that it was a connection, their bodies striving for closeness. Madison wanted to see what it felt like. As his hand slid around her waist, taking possession, she slid her tongue past his lips and into his mouth. Henry's arms tightened at her waist, pulling her closer against him. He tasted like wine and warmth. She was completely lost in sensation. She jumped at a large *clank* from the direction of the waiting carriage.

They broke apart, a chuckle on Henry's lips. "We always seem to be getting interrupted," Henry said with a sigh. He looked over at the carriage with furrowed brows. "I think my sisters are trying to tell us it is time to say goodnight."

Madison tried not to look at the carriage; she had completely forgotten his sisters were waiting only a few yards away. "That did sound suspiciously like the carriage door," Madison observed sheepishly.

Henry shook his head, rolling his eyes. He turned back to Madison, whose hand he still held. Slowly he brought it to his lips. Instead of his customary kiss, he placed one soft kiss on each knuckle, lingering as if he could not quite bring himself to say farewell. "Goodnight, Maddie," he said softly.

"Goodnight Henry." Madison sighed. She missed the warmth of his hand in hers the minute he stepped away. She wanted to stand and watch the carriage pull away, but worried if she did she might not be able to let him go. Wistfully she turned to the front door and let herself inside the townhouse.

Inside the foyer, she removed Denise's borrowed cloak and set it with her reticule and evening gloves on the table. As she did, a maid emerged from the back of the house carrying a tea tray. Madison frowned. "Is my mother still awake?" She asked.

"I do not think so, Miss Hutton," the young woman said, continuing towards the sitting room. "I am bringing tea for Lady Avery," she explained.

"Lady Avery?" Madison hurried around the corner, leaving her things forgotten in the foyer. "Leonora!"

After an awkward afternoon with Eve and an enjoyable but uncomfortably damp evening trying to impress Henry's sisters, Madison was relieved to see Leonora. Denise and Erica had been perfectly kind and cordial, but Madison was keen enough to realize she was being evaluated.

Madison fell gratefully into her older sister's arms. Ten years her senior, the child of their father's first marriage, Leanora had always been a sort of guardian angel in Madison's life. "Apparently this is a day for sisters," she said into her sister's hair, feeling tears well up in her eyes.

"Maddie, I am so glad to see you," Leonora said genuinely, cupping her sister's cheeks and placing a kiss on each. "It was a long trip from Cornwall, but I could not imagine going to bed without seeing you. I rang for tea to keep myself awake."

"Thank you for making the trip, I know it was short notice." The two women sat down on the sofa, their hands clasped affectionately. "Meera is not coming."

Leonora squeezed her sister's hands. "Try not to be too mad at her, dear. She is afraid."

"Christopher is in Spain," Madison said, lips pursed in annoyance.

"But Meera does not know that." Leonora reached up to push back a stray hair from Madison's cheek. "This is an interesting look for an evening at the opera. I am shocked your mother let you leave the house like this."

Madison snorted. "It is a long story. My coiffure was much more appropriate when I left the house."

Leonora's eyebrows shot up. "And what exactly were you up to that had your hair undone?"

Madison rolled her eyes. "Nothing like that, I assure you. Henry and I were with his elder sisters the entire evening. But …" she paused, realizing she had an opportunity here. Her parents were abed, the servants were also mostly retired for the night. She had her elder sister, one of the few society women she respected, alone. "Leonora, can I ask you something?"

"Of course –"

"—about marriage," Madison finished. Leonora cocked an eyebrow, clearly interested.

Madison was not sure how to start, but she was not going to waste this opportunity. "I am very attracted to Henry." Leonora looked amused, but she did not say anything. Madison continued: "And I believe he is very attracted to me."

Hoping her sister would say something, Madison paused. But Leonora just sipped her tea and waited expectantly. Madison sighed. "Henry is kind, he is loyal, he is funny. I feel I can truly be myself with him," she continued. Leonora just sipped her tea.

"Aren't you going to say anything?" Madison crossed her arms in frustration.

"You seem to be saying quite a lot," Leonora observed. "But I haven't heard a question yet."

"I wanted a love match."

"I think we all knew that." Leonora bit her lip to keep her laugh in.

Madison nodded, wringing her hands. "Everything with Henry is just perfect, Leonora. It has been like a dream ... and yet ... he has not told me that he loves me."

Leonora set down her teacup, reaching over and separating Madison's hands so she held each one palm-up in her own. "What makes you think he does not?" She asked seriously.

"He has not said so," Madison said, thinking the answer obvious.

"Men are not as good at expressing their feelings as women are, Madison. Nor at even recognizing them." As she spoke, Leonora gently massaged the palms of her sister's hands, trying to get her to relax. "What has he said to you?"

"He calls me 'love,'" she said. Leonora waited, so Madison continued. "He asked for us to be married right away, as soon as the banns can be read. He has called me beautiful, special, incomparable. He tells me to be myself."

Leonora nodded thoughtfully. "Do those sound to you like the words of a man who is not in love?" She challenged.

"I don't know!" Madison threw her hands up in frustration. Leonora just smiled and caught them again.

"Do you love him?" Leonora asked.

"I think so," she said, then nodded her head more confidently. "Yes, I do."

"Well, Madison, it sounds to me like you are getting everything you ever wanted." Leonora released her hands.

Madison folded them in her lap, her shoulders relaxing. "You think so?"

"I do," Leonora said, giving her sister's shoulder a reassuring squeeze. "Based on the show that the two of you put on out on the front steps a few minutes ago, I think you can feel quite confident about the mutual attraction part."

Madison blushed crimson.

Chapter 11

*T*heodore entered the room not quite knowing what to expect. Henry had been largely absentee the last few weeks, busy squiring around his fiancée and his sisters. But the moment of no return was approaching. Tomorrow was his wedding day.

He found his friend seated behind the desk in his study, all ledgers and paperwork pushed to the side, a tall pour of scotch in front of him. He knew what Henry had been working on; the only tasks Henry had continued to prioritize in the past few weeks were those directly related to the tax reform proposals. But it seemed that on the eve of his wedding, Henry had laid aside even those concerns.

"I was surprised to get your note," Theo said, taking a seat in one of the chairs across from the desk.

"How did you think I would be spending my last night of freedom?" Henry asked with a grin, sitting up to pour a glass for Theo.

"A little less free, I'll admit." Theo accepted the glass, taking a drink and then leaning back casually as well.

"It was hard to shake off my sisters," Henry said, looking apprehensively into the hallway from where Theo had come. "Kick the door closed, would you?"

"The master of the house, hiding in his study." Theo shook his head as he closed the door.

"When there are women in the house, I have no power at all," Henry said truthfully.

"Well then, you had better get used to the feeling."

"You have a point there," Henry acknowledged, lifting a toast to Theo. "But Madison is different."

Theo raised his eyebrows skeptically. "She cannot be that different."

"You've barely talked to her," Henry admonished. "Once we're married, you're going to have to get to know her. She won't give you a choice."

"What an appealing picture you paint."

"You will like her, I promise," Henry said loyally.

"Don't you have any doubts?" Theodore said, clearly struggling to wrap his mind around the whole idea.

"None at all," Henry said easily. Seeing the look of consternation on his friend's face, Henry couldn't help but laugh. "It's just marriage, my friend. It's not the end of the world."

"That's what you think," Theo said darkly. Henry decided not to press. He knew about the skeletons in Theo's closet and he also knew this was not the time to resurrect them.

Deciding it was time to turn the conversation to lighter topics, he raised his glass: "Anyways, I have the wedding night to look forward to. Let's drink to that," he said with a grin.

Theo accepted the invitation and raised his glass. Both men took a deep drink.

"How is the new horse shaping up?" Henry asked as he refilled his glass.

"He's got a bit of an attitude, but I think he will be worth the investment. You should come by and have a look." Theodore accepted the proffered bottle and replenished his drink.

"Well, I am rather busy tomorrow," Henry said jokingly, "But the day after, I will be there. My sisters will be off and I will be back to a normal routine."

"I'll drink to that." Theodore raised his glass, they clinked them together, and drank again.

Madison sat in the carriage across from her mother and father as it bumped along to the church. The sun was shining on a cold and bright spring morning. All morning, her mother had been giving her reassuring squeezes, telling her it was fine to be nervous, it was normal for a bride, on and on … But Madison was not nervous. She had decided to take Leonora's words to heart; Henry had done everything right. He might not be ready to profess his love yet, but his actions had shown he had feelings for her. *The love is there*, she told herself. It was like the blooming buds of spring outside the windows: young, new, just starting to unfurl itself.

So, she was not nervous. She was exhilarated. The carriage came to a halt and Anne jumped skittishly. Her calm of the previous month had deserted her today. Harold took her hand and helped her down from the carriage, glancing over at Madison and rolling his eyes as he did so. Madison chuckled. It was so typical of her parents. Perhaps in twenty years, she and Henry would be at this same church getting ready to watch their own daughter or son be married. *A daughter or son who will have grown up with their own example of love and partnership to look up to.* Madison sighed happily.

Leonora was waiting outside the carriage. "You look lovely," she said, taking Madison's hand and pressing a kiss to her cheek. Leonora turned to her stepmother, Anne. "Shall we go in?" She asked, offering her arm.

Anne looked at Madison, but for once in her life seemed unable to find any words. Instead, she gave her daughter a quick kiss on the cheek, looped her arm through Leonora's, and went into the church before she lost control of her emotions.

Harold shook his head at his departing wife, then turned back to his daughter. "You can still make a run for it if you want," he offered.

Madison shook her head. "I think I will stay," she said with a smile.

"Alright then. A father has to try." He took her hand and squired her inside the church, his own eyes misty.

Down the long aisle of the church, Madison saw Henry waiting. His hair had gotten longer since they met. His shiny brown locks touched the neck of his coat. Madison imagined running her hands through it, feeling the thickness between her fingers. *Such thoughts*, she admonished herself. *And in a church, no less.* But her heart beat faster and faster as she walked down the aisle to her future.

Henry was uncomfortably aware of how fast his own heart was beating. Theo had asked him the night before if he had any doubts. It was true, he had none. Madison was everything he had hoped to find in a wife and marchioness. And as she floated down the aisle towards him, he could not help but think himself the luckiest man in the world.

She was wearing a pale blue gown, carefully ruched organza at the top, but soft and flowy from the waist down. A silver sash heavily encrusted with sparkling gems was tied just below her bust. A long silver necklace hung around her neck, its large diamond pendant nestled between her breasts. Her beautiful hair was fully down. Henry had not realized how long it was; the strands reached down past her elbows. It should have made her look younger, more juvenile, but it had the complete opposite effect. She looked like a Roman goddess: confident, free, assured of her power and prowess. The only adornment was a headband, encrusted with jewels that matched her sash.

As her father kissed each of her cheeks and stepped away, leaving her with him, Henry felt like his entire world had fallen into place. He could not keep the smile off of his face. Madison met his gaze with a radiant smile of her own. When they turned to the bishop to begin the ceremony, neither of them could imagine a more perfect moment.

Throughout the welcome, readings, and sermon, they both recited and bowed their heads just as they were expected to do. But beyond that Henry made little pretense of focusing on the clergyman; his eyes were on Madison the entire time. Madison was surprised when she cast a sidelong glance his way only to find that he was watching her intently.

The air between them was thick with anticipation. This was the moment they had been building to for weeks. For Madison, it was the moment she had envisioned her entire life. When they finally came to the vows, her heart was beating so fast she was sure it would explode from inside her chest. Henry repeated his vows unflinchingly, a half-cocked smile on his face. When the bishop turned to Madison, her tongue felt like it weighed a thousand pounds inside her mouth. She opened it, but no sound came out. The bishop looked at her expectantly, but Madison was frozen.

Holding back a laugh, Henry threw tradition to the wind and took her hand. The bishop looked thoroughly offended; the couple need not touch until the rings were exchanged. But Madison felt warmth flood through her from where their hands joined, through her stomach, chest, and heart.

When she opened her mouth again to speak, the words came smoothly: "I, Madison Anne Elizabeth Hutton, take thee, Henry Arnold William Warsham, to be my wedded Husband, to have and to hold from this day forward, for better for worse, for richer for poorer, in sickness and in health, to love, cherish, and to obey, till death us do part, according to God's holy ordinance; and thereto I give thee my troth."

They moved to the exchange of rings, and as Henry slid the wedding band onto her finger he recited the words: "With this Ring I thee wed, with my body I thee worship," he paused just for a moment, the inflection slightly different as he spoke the word *worship*. Then he finished: "And with all my worldly goods I thee endow: In the name of the

Father, and of the Son, and of the Holy Ghost. Amen."

It was done. The ceremony continued with the blessing, proclamation, and communion, but Madison barely noticed it. Hundreds, perhaps even thousands, of men and women had stood before this altar and proclaimed a union founded on love. But for she and Henry, it would be true. A true love match.

Chapter 12

*L*ooking back, Madison hardly remembered how she got from the altar back to her parents' townhouse for their wedding breakfast. The only thing that stuck in her memory was the feeling of heat wherever Henry's body touched hers. He held her hand in his arm as he escorted her back down the aisle. His leg was pressed against hers in the carriage as they drove away from the church. His lips touched hers in long, lingering kisses that filled the time between ceremony and reception. As they stood in her parents' foyer, greeting guests, he kept one hand pressed to the small of her back. And when they sat down to breakfast with the assembled guests, his hand found her knee under the table.

Madison's eyes flew up in surprise, landing on his face. To all other onlookers Henry looked perfectly serene, nodding along as he spoke to Madison's father, who was seated on his other side. But Madison saw the hint of a smile at the corner of his lips. She tried to keep her face as well-trained as his, but then he started stroking his hand up and down along her thigh. It wasn't particularly intimate, she supposed, but she had certainly never been touched that way by another person, let alone a man. *By her husband*, she thought to herself, a little breathless at the thought.·

"Madison, are you alright?" Erica asked. She was seated a few spots away from Madison and was giving her the most peculiar look.

"Yes! Yes, of course," Madison said, turning away from Henry resolutely and looking at his sister. "Did you say something?"

"I was commenting on how lovely your parents' home here in London is," Erica said, glancing between her brother and his new wife suspiciously. She pursed her lips into a little half-smile but did not offer further comment.

"Thank you," Madison said. Henry had changed tactics, now using his fingertips to draw tantalizing little circles along the top of her thigh. "They rented it for the Season. We don't typically spend much time in London."

"*We* will though, my love," Henry interjected, giving Madison a sweet and innocent smile.

Madison forced herself to take a deep breath. Her heart was hammering in her chest. Deciding to take control of matters, she slid her hand from underneath her napkin and caught his. "Yes, indeed *we* will," she said, gripping his hand tightly in her own and giving him a reproving look.

Henry laughed, surrendering to his wife gracefully. "Erica, do you plan on staying in London much longer yourself?" He asked his sister pointedly.

Denise, seated next to her sister, cut in: "We will be staying a few weeks longer, dear brother. We've made the trip; best to make use of it and accomplish errands and such. I've brought my girls' measurements, so I can have new gowns made."

"But we will not be lodging with you any longer," Erica interjected. "We will be staying with my husband's sister and her family. You will have some privacy." She sent a pointed look at her sister, who had clearly left this detail out just to rile her brother.

Madison felt a mix of relief and anxiety. She was glad for the opportunity to get to know Henry's sisters, but she also did not want them watching over her every waking move during her first few days and weeks as his marchioness. However, with Denise and Erica staying elsewhere, Madison and Henry would be alone in that huge mansion. Now that they were married, all Madison could think about was what came next. Clearly, Henry's mind was there also. The notion of spending the next several days alone with Henry … anxiety and anticipation did not adequately describe how she felt … she was nearly vibrating.

When breakfast adjourned, the guests filed out into the other parts of the house, lingering over glasses of champagne. Madison found herself standing alone against a wall, much as she had the evening of her first ball. The evening when she had met Henry. She had wondered that night if she would be able to find the man she was looking for among the throngs of dandies, fortune-hunters, and fools. And here she was, less than two months later, a married woman. She must have looked overwhelmed because Denise appeared from the crowd with a reassuring smile.

Denise handed Madison a glass of champagne. "Take a breath, dear, the hard part is over now." Madison accepted it with a grateful smile, feeling the warm glow of acceptance as Henry's eldest sister squeezed her hand before departing to speak to another guest. She was Madison Warsham now, she reminded herself. She was part of the family.

Henry came up alongside her, leaning in close to whisper in her ear: "I think it is time for us to go." Madison jumped in surprise, finding Henry unexpectedly looking down at her from over her shoulder. She turned her face up towards his. His fingers lightly touched the sensitive skin behind her ear, sending shivers through her.

"Alright, yes." Madison nodded, flooded with an eagerness she did not quite understand but could not wait another moment to explore. "I am ready."

The trip from her parents' townhouse to the mansion Madison and Henry would now call home passed in a flash. They did not talk much. Neither of them knew what to say, especially in the forced proximity of the carriage. It took every ounce of self-control that Henry possessed to sit next to her, holding her hand, and nothing more. He was afraid that if he did so much as kiss her now, without the eyes of society watching, he would take full advantage of her willing innocence.

She could feel how tense Henry was, taut as a bowstring. His easy smile had faded, replaced by occasional heated glances but mostly by determined staring out the window. But he was still holding her hand. He was holding it rather tightly. That reassured her that nothing was amiss.

When the carriage came to a halt, Henry jumped out of it so quickly Madison expected to find him sprawled on the ground outside. However, he had landed adeptly and was waiting with his hand outstretched. "Are you ready to come home, my little marchioness?" He asked with a grin.

Madison couldn't help the girlish giggle that escaped her. "Please do not let anyone hear you saying that. I don't need that to be my new *ton* nickname."

She took his hand and climbed down carefully. The footboard of the carriage was ornately carved with vines and leaves wrapped around his family crest. She had not noticed it before, though she had now taken several trips in this carriage. She would soon know all these little details by heart, she realized. This was her home. As she gripped Henry's hand, she looked up at the expansive mansion with new eyes.

Henry tucked her hand into his arm. Instead of taking her into the house, he led her along the covered walkway the encircled the courtyard. "I did not know you were sensitive about your height," he said, a singular eyebrow quirked.

Making a show of looking up at him, Madison wrinkled her nose. "I am not, usually." She hoped he would lean down and kiss her, a feat she could not accomplish on her own because of their height differential. But Henry just smiled wanly down at her. Sinking back down from her tip-toes, she let out an almost imperceptible sigh. "I am sure the society gossips will have plenty to say about me. I suppose if they are only commenting on my height, that is not such a bother."

"I think the society gossips have learned their lesson after that little show you put on a few weeks ago," Henry said. They continued to walk through the stone archways, around the side of the house, until the pathway opened into the extensive gardens at the rear of the mansion.

Madison smiled wickedly. "That was rather enjoyable, watching those catty ladies squirm. But if you think they are the worst of London's gossips, then you are woefully naïve."

"Woefully naïve?" Henry laughed. "That is not a charge I have ever before had laid at my door."

"You're welcome," Madison said with an impish smile.

Henry was completely taken with her. He was purposefully trying to keep the conversation jocular and light-hearted. If he let it get any more serious or heady, he might sweep her up in his arms and carry her to the bedroom before midday.

Madison saw the flash of desire in his eyes. It was the same look he had when he had been caressing her leg beneath the table. He tried to mask it, and he almost succeeded. But she was becoming more adept at reading his expressions. Her heart leapt up into her throat. The hours between now and the wedding night seemed infinite.

"Thank you, please give my compliments to …" Madison trailed off, looking to Henry questioningly.

"Mrs. Palin," he said, supplying the name of his cook.

"Mrs. Palin," Madison repeated, determined to commit the name to memory.

The butler and footman departed with bows and blushes. Henry shook his head as he watched them go. Madison had been busy charming his staff all day. He had shown her every inch of the London estate, inside and out. She had even smiled along gamely as he showed her through the stables, which he knew held little interest for her. And they had finally arrived here: at the conclusion of their evening meal.

"What do you customarily do in the evenings?" Madison glanced around the deserted dining room, suddenly very aware of how alone they were. All day, she had been acutely aware of how often they were left alone. In the carriage, in the hallways, in the library. Her entire life, she had been chaperoned and her reputation staunchly protected. And with a few words, a simple exchange of vows, she was now permitted a whole new kind of freedom.

"I am usually not here in the evenings," Henry said honestly. Madison nodded. Obviously, he would attend various social engagements most evenings during the Season, the same as she would. Not sure what to do next, Madison looked around the room, at her hands, everywhere but at Henry.

"There is one room you haven't seen yet."

Madison's stomach completely flipped over. She forced air in and out of her lungs. Henry's eyes were on her now, and she did not look away. She nodded, too breathless to say anything at all.

Needing no further invitation, Henry stood. He closed the few feet between them, taking her hand and drawing her to her feet. Slowly, purposefully, he drew her hand to his mouth and placed a kiss on every single knuckle. Madison's hand tingled, a warmth that spread down her arm, into her chest and heart. Henry kept her hand close at his lips and drew her closer. Then he leaned down and kissed her lips. His kiss was feather-light at first, really several small kisses across her lips like he had across her hand. Then his free hand caught the back of her neck and pulled her closer to him, deepening the kiss.

Madison gave free rein to her feelings. His mouth was hot and intoxicating against hers. When his tongue slowly slid into her mouth, she met it with her own. She had no sense of time passing, but she could feel the urgency building in her own body. She arched against him, a primal need to be close to him taking hold. Henry moaned.

He broke away. Before Madison could question him, he swept her up into his arms, hooking her hand around his neck and his arm under her knees. She felt an exhilarated laugh bubble out of her as he quickly crossed the room, pushing open the door with his shoulder and taking long strides down the hallway towards the stairs.

"This is a different view," Madison said cheekily. Henry paused at the bottom of the stairway, leaning down to kiss her soundly. When he pulled back, he was satisfied by her dreamy-eyed look and continued up to the next floor.

Henry stopped in front of the door to a room they had not entered earlier. When showing her the upper floors, he had waved down the hallway and indicated that the lord and lady's chambers were located in the eastern wing of the house. In reality, he hadn't dared show her their apartments. He did not trust himself not to take her to bed immediately.

The room they entered had a huge fireplace, which the servants had done up with a roaring fire. Two sofas faced each other and a large arched window that overlooked the gardens in the daytime. Now all that was visible were the twinkling stars.

Carrying her over the threshold, Henry continued through two more open doors which adjoined another sitting room. The furniture in this one was noticeably more delicate and feminine. This room was meant for the marchioness.

Madison forced herself to swallow the lump in her throat before she spoke.

"Can I just ... have a couple of moments to myself? I will be right along, I promise."

Henry felt like he had been hit over the head. *Damn, would she ever stop surprising him?* He lowered her to the ground slowly, setting her back on her feet. He motioned deeper into the room, to the doorway beyond, where a large bed was just visible in the candlelight.

"These are your apartments now. You are Lady Warsham." He was pleased to see her small smile as she looked around the room. She squeezed his hand, and he fought the urge to pick her up and carry her over to the bed straight away.

"If you need some time –" he started, but she cut him off, reaching up and kissing him. A kiss full of invitation.

"I just need a moment," she whispered against his lips.

He forced air down into his lungs and nodded. "The door there connects to my rooms." He pointed to the heavy wooden door back through the joint sitting room. "I will wait for you." He moved toward the door, reluctant to let go of her hand. "Don't take too long." Henry saw the mixed look of amusement and anticipation on her face but closed the door behind him before he lost all his resolve.

Walking into what would now be her bedroom, Madison saw that her trunks had been delivered but not unpacked. Perched on top of the stack was a smaller bag she had packed herself after her mother and her maid had left the room. Opening the clasp and pulling out the shimmering garment within, she felt a shiver of sensation slide down her spine. *Now or never*, she thought to herself.

Henry's heart stopped. He could not breathe. He was sure the world had just stopped moving altogether.

She looked like a moonbeam.

Her long blonde hair was brushed out and flowing over her shoulders. Beneath the long waves of white gold, she wore a confection of silvery lace as fine as a spiderweb.

Two long panels of silver lace were draped over her shoulders, skimming the edges of her breasts and stomach and thighs to reach the ground. They met in a deep V just above her navel, where they were secured with a silk tie cinched around her waist. The curve of her hip was adorned only with the silver silk tie that held the lace in place. He could see every inch of her graceful legs.

Madison watched Henry's reaction closely. He did not speak, but she was beginning to realize that his words deserting him was not necessarily a bad sign. She walked slowly through the doorway and across the room. Henry was standing next to the bed, his shirt halfway unbuttoned. His waistcoat had already been discarded on the floor next to him. When she stopped in front of him, Madison saw him take in a deep breath, his chest rising and falling emphatically. Beneath the open buttons of his shirt, she could see the smattering of hair, a few shades darker than the hair on his head. Fascinated to feel it for herself, she reached out and touched her hand to his chest. The dark curls were softer than she expected, and his body was burning.

As she slid her hand up his chest, she felt his sharp inhale. With a boldness her virginity could not account for, she unbuttoned his shirt and pulled it over his head so that he stood bare-chested before her. Madison had never seen a fully-grown man shirtless and up close. He was a masterpiece. She ran her hands up his arms, gripping his shoulders and massaging the muscles with her thumbs, exploring the way they felt beneath her fingers.

When she lifted her arms to his shoulders, her breasts lifted also, the dark circles rising into view beneath the lacework. Henry could not hold back a moment longer. He took possession of her shoulders, slid his hands down her waist, and lifted her so her lips met his.

Madison was eager and ready. She leaned against him, allowing him to lift her off her feet. Their bodies were pressed together from toe to navel to lips; Madison could not touch the ground even if she tried. But holding her in place, Henry could not explore her body. And he wanted to worship every curve he felt pressed against him.

He turned towards the bed, lowering her down gently to the soft mattress. For just a moment, they broke apart. Their faces were inches from each other's, their eyes locked. Madison reached up and brushed away a strand of his light brown hair, longer now than it had been in memory, which had fallen over his brow. Henry turned his head and pressed a kiss to her wrist. And then another. He trailed kisses down her arm until he reached her mouth, which he took without hesitation.

Both horizontal now on the bed, Henry's hands were free to explore the delectable confection Madison had presented. He ran one finger down the center of her chest, not touching her breasts. Madison arched her back, not knowing what she wanted, exactly, but knowing that whatever it was she wanted it desperately. Henry drew his hand downward, to where the lace garment was tied. With one hand, he untied the silk ribbon, and with the other he pulled away the layers of lace to reveal Madison's expanses of creamy skin. For a long minute he just looked at her, completely transfixed.

Madison watched Henry's face. It was unreadable to her inexperienced eyes. But his eyes were dark; so much darker than she had ever seen them. Not knowing what else to do, she reached up, sliding her hand into the downy-soft hairs at the nape of his neck, and drew him to her.

The trance broken, Henry allowed his hands to freely explore her body while his mouth explored hers. He slid his hands downward, catching her breasts in his palms. He felt the shiver that went through her. No one had ever touched her like this, and though the feelings were new, the way she moaned into his mouth reassured him that she was enjoying it. His hands working in perfect tandem, he flicked a fingertip over each of her nipples. The sound that Madison – a gasp, a moan, a cry, all tangled into one – reverberated through him. Desperate to hear the unadulterated sounds of her pleasure, he released her mouth and slid his tongue along the pale, delicate column of her neck.

As his tongue traced seductive spirals along her neck, his hands continued their amorous assault of her breasts. Madison did not try to contain the sensations and sounds spilling out of her. No one had told her that lovemaking would be like this – a cascading explosion of feeling that just kept building and building. While Henry's tongue and lips touched every sensitive part of her neck and throat, his hands teased and caressed. His touch was soft and then firmer. The barely discernable floating of fingertips over her breast, and then the sharper scrape of a fingernail over her ultra-sensitive nipples. She cried out, arching her hips upward. She wanted something, needed it urgently, but she did not know what. "Henry …" she said, her voice almost pleading.

Through the fog of arousal and desire, Henry heard her voice and the plea in it. She did not know what she was asking for, but he did. He slid his hands from her breasts down to her hips. As his fingers stroked the elegant line from her hip to her navel, his lips came back to hers. Madison felt his hands lift away from her and realized he was removing his trousers. When he moved his weight fully back onto the bed, there were no more barriers between them.

Not sure what to expect, Madison raised herself onto her elbows and chanced a glance downward.

Her eyes widened; that could not possibly be reasonable. She looked at him in complete shock. Henry was torn between a laugh and a groan. "It's alright," he assured her.

Madison opened her mouth to protest, but Henry caught her mouth with his and any words she had died on her lips. She trusted Henry completely. He slid his hand down her body, to the apex of her desire, and urged her legs apart.

She knew what was going to happen next, and was bracing herself for the flash of pain that she had been warned about. There was the briefest pinch as Henry entered her, but it faded away instantly, completely overwhelmed by the feeling of fullness and connection. They were truly joined, she realized, as their bodies began to move together.

Henry tried hard to hold himself together. She was perfect. Every inch of her porcelain skin, the way her blonde hair had darkened at her temples as her desire manifested itself in physical perspiration – all of it just made his desire for her grow. When he finally entered her, it felt like coming home; as if every moment between them had been building to this one. He almost lost himself immediately, totally taken over by his desire for her. But the look on her face, the way she wrinkled her brow, the soft little moans she was emitting without even realizing it, helped him hold on. He wanted her to truly understand and feel their joining.

She bit her lip, then sank her teeth in harder, and then her mouth opened and she moaned: a long, primitive sound that she would not even recall making the next morning. Henry knew she was reaching her climax. He reached down and caught her hand in his, gripping it tightly, lacing their fingers together. She cried out again as the waves of pleasure crashed over her. When he felt the last tremor echo through her body, he finally let himself go.

They lay there in the bed for a long time without speaking, their legs and arms entangled. Madison had no words to describe what Henry had just given her. Henry had no idea how a virgin could inspire such depth of feeling within him. Instead of talking, they turned to each other and met in a long, slow kiss that said everything they could not.

Chapter 13

When she woke up the next morning, Madison was momentarily disoriented. Above her were not the familiar ceiling panels of her bedroom in her parents' home, but rather the silk draperies of a canopied bed. Slowly she sat up and looked around the room; her new room, she reminded herself. The room was decorated in rose and gold, the colors she had picked weeks ago. The bed she laid in was huge, much bigger than the one she was accustomed to sleeping in. Well, this one wasn't *just* for sleeping, she thought with a slightly embarrassed smile.

In addition to the huge bed, there was a chaise in front of the fireplace, and two doors that opened to a small sitting room outfitted with matching furnishings. Through there was another door, which she had learned last night led to Henry's apartments.

Where was Henry? Her memory of the night was a haze of sensations and lovemaking. At some point she recalled falling asleep in his arms, feeling completely safe and satisfied. But she had woken up alone. Thinking he must have gone to his rooms to fetch something and eager to see him, Madison got up from the bed. Looking down, she realized she was naked with a no-longer-virginal blush. She glanced to her trunks, stacked along one wall. Sorting through those would be a nightmare. So instead she conscripted one of the sheets from the bed, wrapping it around her body and securing it with a little knot just above her breasts.

She opened the doors to her sitting room. The fire was alight; the servants had already been in this morning. The door that connected her sitting room to Henry's was also closed. Madison frowned. How long had he been gone for?

As Madison opened the door, she expected to find Henry - perhaps he was sitting having his morning tea. But again, she was met with emptiness. There was one more door to try: the one to his bedroom. When she opened it, both she and the valet jumped in surprise.

"I beg your pardon, my lady," the valet bowed and backed away, clearly discomfited by her attire. Madison blushed and retreated automatically towards the door. But she was not entirely deterred.

"I am looking for Lord Warsham," she said with as much dignity as someone wrapped in a sheet could manage.

The middle-aged valet was blushing and trying to keep his eyes downcast so as not to look at the barely-clad lady of the house. "I believe his lordship has gone down for the day, my lady," the poor man managed to say.

Madison felt her mouth drop open in surprise, but then hastily closed it. She smiled and nodded serenely. "Thank you, sir. Please go about your business."

Holding her head high, she left the bedroom and closed the door behind her. Sinking into one of the plush dark velvet chairs in Henry's sitting room, Madison frowned. It seemed quite unusual for a man, on the morning after his wedding, to be anywhere other than with his wife. It was not exactly how she had pictured the start of their honeymoon period.

Henry had been a bachelor in this house for many years, Madison reminded herself. It was only natural he would have established rituals and routines. She would just have to insert herself into them, she thought with a smile. With a nod of determination, she returned to her room and rang for a maid.

Thirty minutes later she was descending the stairs into the grand hall. The frocks her mother had commissioned for her trousseau were truly gorgeous. The maid had helped her select a rich primrose purple colored dress that was edged with matching lace. The peek of lace along the neckline drew attention to her bosom and the trim on the cap sleeves accentuated the spring look perfectly. Madison even let the maid weave a matching ribbon through her plaited hair. She felt like a queen as she floated through the ornately decorated halls of the mansion.

Her step quickened as she walked through the house, her excitement to find her husband fizzing in her like champagne. She peeked into the morning room. That was where her parents usually took a casual breakfast. It was empty. He must be in the dining room. Madison's search was rewarded: Henry sat at the head of the long, highly polished cherry wood table.

Henry's eyes lit and he smiled immediately when she entered the room. "Good morning, my love," he said, standing up to pull out a chair for her.

Madison was thrilled when he pulled out the seat next to him. For a moment, when she found him seated in the formal dining room, she thought he might expect her to sit at the complete other end of the table opposite him. Maybe that was what was expected for a marquess and marchioness. Pleased that she did not have to relieve him of that notion, Madison took her seat happily.

"You look lovely this morning," Henry said without preamble, his meaning obvious. He caught Madison's eye, and the heat there sent a blush of desire right through her.

"Thank you," Madison said, her eyes locked on his. She thought he was going to lean over and kiss her right there in the dining room. She would certainly have let him. But then a footman entered with a tray of offerings and Madison swallowed the impulse.

"It was quite a hunt to find you this morning," Madison said as she accepted a cup of tea from the footman. "Just a bit of cream and sugar, please," she said, smiling at the young man and reminding herself she must set to learning the names of all the staff as soon as possible.

"I did not know you were a morning person," Henry said, drinking his tea. He was fascinated watching her. Every movement made him want to take her to bed. The way she cocked her head to the side when she thanked the footman for her tea highlighted the long column of her neck. He wanted to run his tongue along it and feel her shiver delightfully beneath him.

She was a vixen. An unexpected revelation. He had known he was attracted to her, but last night the overwhelming ferocity of that attraction had taken him by surprise. Then she showed up in the dining room looking like that ... she was going to make it damn hard to go about his day.

"Are you reading that?" Madison asked.

Henry was confused. Then he saw her looking at the stack of daily news sheets on the silver tray to his left. He lifted the top one off and offered it to her. "By all means," he said.

She rewarded him with a bright smile, setting the paper in front of her and starting to read as she sipped her tea. Henry watched her with interest for a few minutes. He had never met a woman who read the morning periodicals. But she was genuinely absorbed, her eyes moving from left to right as she read along the columns.

The headlines were dominated by the movement for income tax repeal. There had been a public meeting that had turned riotous only a few days earlier. That was the main reason for the stack of newspapers. Henry was trying to keep a pulse on the matter by reading the daily news sheets from all over the city, and beyond when he could get them. Confining his reading to periodicals targeted at the nobility would not give him a broad enough view of public sentiment. He was certainly surprised to see Madison so absorbed. He had never seen a woman interested in public affairs, let alone something as mundane and complicated as tax policy. After a few minutes, he picked up another newspaper from the stack and started reading himself.

Madison was in heaven. They were sitting in companionable silence, eating breakfast and sipping tea while they read the morning news. Every once in a while, she caught Henry watching her over the top of his news sheet, and she met his gaze with a bold smile. The look in his eyes was causing memories of the previous evening to flood her mind. She felt a blush rising up her cheeks.

Henry laid down his paper and leaned across the table. He casually ran a finger along her hand, wrist, and up her forearm. Madison felt her heartbeat start to speed up.

"You're making it extremely difficult to concentrate on what I am reading," she said with a breathless smile.

"Am I?" Henry's hand was on her shoulder now, toying with the end of her long plait of golden hair. When his fingertips skittered along the nape of her neck, she put down her newspaper and any pretense of reading.

They were so close together, she realized. *How had that happened?* They were like magnets moving towards one another. Madison closed her eyes, knowing his lips would touch hers any moment —

"Excuse me, my lord –"

Madison jumped backward as the butler entered the room. Henry stayed exactly where he was, leaning far forward across the table, resting on one elbow. He was unconcerned about the thoughts or sensibilities of their butler.

"You asked for your horse to be saddled and ready at ten," the butler said.

Henry chuckled. *Damn*, this wife of his would have him completely wrapped around her finger before either of them realized it. He had completely forgotten his appointment. Indeed, a minute before he had every intention of carrying Madison back upstairs to their apartments for a proper 'good morning.'

Instead, he nodded at his butler. "Of course. I will be along momentarily." He turned back to Madison. "I will see *you* this evening," he said, his eyes and tone rich with implication.

Madison was genuinely confused. "You are leaving?" She asked disbelievingly.

"I have an appointment with my solicitor this morning," Henry confirmed, standing up and straightening himself.

"And then...?" Madison looked up at him, eyebrows raised.

"Lunch at my club, some parliamentary business this afternoon, and so on." He nodded to the newspaper in her hand. "The income tax repeal you have been reading about is consuming both Houses of Parliament. But I will try to make it to whichever social event you have chosen for this evening."

"I haven't chosen anything," Madison said. "I thought –"

"No need to delay on my account. I know how much you enjoy the social whirl." Henry smiled and winked. Then he leaned down and kissed her on the cheek. His hand lingered on her shoulder. He leaned back down and kissed her again, this time full on the lips. When he didn't feel her respond, he found himself smiling internally. For all that Madison was a rebel, until last night she had been a proper, virginal bride. It would take time for her to get used to these casual physical exchanges.

He gave her shoulder a final squeeze and then headed for the door. "Have a good day, my love," he said over his shoulder.

Madison had hardly been the Marchioness of Clydon for twenty-four hours, and now she was sitting at a dining table that could seat thirty, in an expansive mansion, completely alone. This was not the honeymoon she had pictured.

Madison sat at the breakfast table for a long time. It was only when a servant came into the room to clean and jumped in surprise, clearly not expecting to find the room occupied, that Madison realized the time. She glanced at the clock; it was nearing midday. She excused herself awkwardly, wandering into the great hall. She looked upon the majestic entry hall with new eyes. When she first arrived here, fresh from formalizing their courtship, she had been awed by the grandeur. This morning she allowed herself to peruse the room more slowly. She looked at each individual painting that hung on the walls. Some were landscapes; many were life-size portraits. Henry's relatives? She wondered. Surely, they must be.

She spent several hours exploring the long halls and elegant rooms of the house. Although Henry had given her a thorough tour the day before, she realized now just how much she had not absorbed. She had been rather distracted by her new husband's sidelong glances and affectionate touches. She was familiar with a few rooms from their time courting; everything else she discovered for herself. The ornate collection of circular windows that overlooked the courtyard were striking. Madison could easily picture herself standing there, watching guests arrive in a flurry of excitement. The library was a particular respite. Isolated from much of the house down the long hallway that overlooked the courtyard, it was quiet and undisturbed.

Finally, after taking her afternoon tea, Madison made her way upstairs. She had little interest in the endless hallways of bedrooms. Perhaps someday she would know the attractions of each, assigning the most desirable to honored guests. But today her focus was elsewhere.

She looked upon the lord and lady's chambers with new eyes. The evening before, and even that morning, she had noted only the palatial elegance of the suite of rooms reserved for each of the marquess and marchioness. She entered through the same doorway Henry had carried her over the night before.

Looking around the marquess' sitting room, she noted the masculine touches: a heavy bookcase laden with thick volumes, chairs upholstered in dark red velvet. Wary after her first visit, she opened Henry's bedroom door slowly. But the room was empty. There was a large four-poster bed, identical in size but more ornately carved than the one in her bedroom. The fireplace was intricately carved to depict a woodland hunting scene. She looked closely at the bed, trying to decide if it had been slept in the night before. But Henry's staff, *their staff*, was thorough and exacting. The bed was tightly made, the pillows plumped, and she had no idea if Henry had left her upon waking or spent some portion of the night asleep in his bed.

With growing disquiet, Madison returned to her rooms. Weeks ago, Henry had asked her what her preferences were for her suite, noting that it was customary to redecorate the rooms for the incoming marchioness. At the time, Madison had found the question sweet. But now she reconsidered. Had he asked her for her preferences because she alone would be spending time in these rooms, and therefore his preferences did not matter? Were the separate sitting rooms, bedrooms, and dressing rooms a nod to tradition…or a norm Henry expected they would fulfill?

She sat and stared at herself aimlessly in the mirror at her dressing table for a long time, her mind working. When she finally rose hours later to dress for supper, she had a plan in her mind.

Henry returned to the house ready for anything. Whether it be ball or opera, soiree or dinner party, he was ready for whatever evening entertainments Madison had selected. All he wanted was to be close to her. She had been on his mind all day. As he sipped scotch at his club, as he discussed the positions offered by both the property owners from Wessex whom he had recently met with and the storekeeper's guild here in London … she was there, beautiful and enticing as ever.

He handed his horse over to the groom eagerly, a strong spring in his step as he climbed the stairs to the house. His butler opened the door with a formal bow.

"Good evening," Henry said, his eyes already looking around the entry hall, searching in earnest for his wife. "Is Lady Warsham upstairs?" Henry asked when he did not find her immediately.

"She is in the dining room, my lord."

Without hesitation, Henry's long strides carried him through the entry hall and into the dining room. He came to an abrupt stop when he entered. Madison was seated in the exact spot he had left her this morning. But instead of her purple day dress, she was garbed in a dark amethyst evening gown. It was suitable for a ball, or perhaps even an audience at court. But instead, she sat at their dining table, smiling at him from across the room.

"I am woefully underdressed," Henry said, looking down at his daytime attire with a self-deprecating smile.

"I think you look wonderful," Madison said, looking him over appreciatively.

"Give me a few minutes to change, and I will join you."

"No, don't go," Madison started to stand, but relaxed when Henry made no actual moves to leave. "Please, it is just the two of us. Join me now," she said, her voice sensuously smooth. As she spoke, she rested her hand on her chest, drawing his eyes to the tantalizing curve of her breasts. Henry was sure it was an innocent gesture, but it inflamed him all the same.

"If you insist," Henry managed to say, noting the strangled quality of his voice.

"I do," Madison said with a coquettish smile.

Henry walked the length of the table and came to sit beside her at the other end of the room. The instant he was seated, the door to the next room opened and the footmen entered with the first course.

Henry watched the food being served, the wine being poured, with a question in his eyes. As the servants retreated, he turned to Madison. "I expected to be heading upstairs to change for the evening. Am I to believe you did not have a slate of entertainments to choose from this evening?"

Madison shook her head as she took a sip of wine. "There were many invitations," she confirmed. "But I hardly think that anyone expects us to accept any of them, so soon after our wedding. We are very much in our honeymoon period, after all."

Henry thought he detected the subtlest shift in the tone of her voice on those last words. He looked at her closely, trying to discern if there was something he ought to comprehend but was missing. But Madison just smiled at him over the rim of her wineglass.

Not sure what else to do, Henry raised his fork and started eating the food laid in front of him. The meal passed unremarkably. Madison asked a few questions about the house, Henry offered a passing comment here and there about his activities during the day. Henry felt himself begin to relax; his discomfiture was for nothing. Madison had simply decided to spend the evening at home. And it was a perfectly enjoyable evening. She looked beautiful, her pale skin shimmering against the deep jewel tones of her gown like an opal.

When the last course was cleared, Henry motioned towards the doors that connected the dining room to the less formal sitting room. "Would you care to adjourn to the sitting room?"

"I suppose," Madison said, following his gaze. But then she glanced meaningfully at the other doorway: the doorway that led to the main hall and the stairway beyond. Henry felt a throbbing begin to take hold, deep in the core of his body.

"Or perhaps we could make our way … upstairs?" He suggested, his voice taking that same odd strangled quality he had observed earlier.

Madison swallowed hard. She felt that fiery tingling starting to spread throughout her body. It was not quite familiar yet, but at least now she knew what it meant. Henry stood, offering her his hand. She stood herself, sliding her hand into his and allowing him to lead her from the room. Her heart was beating like a drum in her chest. All thoughts of the day, worries about his room and hers, were completely eclipsed by the heat radiating from their joined hands.

As soon as the door to her sitting room closed behind them, Henry took her into his arms and kissed her. His mouth was on hers, his hands sliding up her back, his tongue drawing hers into a wild dance. Madison lost all ability for conscious thought. She tangled her fingers in his long, silky hair, thrusting her hips forward unconsciously while her mouth clung to his hungrily. She was not aware of how either of them was relieved of their clothes, just that they were suddenly pressed together skin to skin.

Henry's lips trailed down her neck, across her chest, fixing on one hard nipple. He flicked his tongue over the hard little bud, sending shivers of desire rippling through her. Madison heard herself cry out, a wild, wanton sound she could hardly recognize as her own. He slid his hands under her rounded buttocks; she instinctively wrapped her legs around his waist as he carried her to the bed. They landed on the soft coverlet in a tangle of limbs. Madison was intensely aware of every place his body touched hers.

Henry could not get enough of her. His lips kissed along the sensitive underside of one breast, while his hand gripped the round fullness of her bottom.

He could not hold back any longer. Claiming Madison's lips with his own, he moved so he was fully atop her on the bed. With one stroke, his body joined with hers. Their bodies rocked together. Henry felt himself building quickly. He did not know how long he would be able to hold himself back. Madison moaned, her fingernails digging into his shoulder. Then her cries escalated, a desperate cry as she reached for gratification. The urgency of her desire put Henry over the top, and they crashed towards climax together.

They laid together in her bed, wrapped in each other's arms until the last vestiges of the evening had faded into night. There were no sounds from outside the window. The city outside was settling.

Madison finally felt herself begin to relax. Perhaps she had been overreacting. They had shared a pleasant meal, riotous lovemaking, and now they were ensconced perfectly together. As the moon rose in the sky, she allowed herself to close her eyes and finally drift off to sleep.

But before she could fully relax, she was startled awake by movement beneath her head. Slowly, deliberately, Henry was easing her head off of his chest and onto a pillow. The movement was so gentle, so careful, it could almost have been construed as loving. As he moved slowly off the bed, coming to stand beside the ornately hung four-poster, Henry even pulled up the coverlet and tucked it around her naked body. Then, without a word or an explanation, he turned and walked from the room.

As the door to Henry's chambers closed softly behind him, Madison sat bolt upright in bed. Separate bedrooms, separate lives ... this was not just a nod to tradition. This was the reality Henry expected them to live.

Chapter 14

As the days stretched into weeks, Madison's days took on a familiar and repetitive cadence. She awoke alone. She would ring for her maid, go through her morning ablutions, and go downstairs to the dining room for breakfast. Most mornings, she found Henry seated at the table just as she had on the first morning of their marriage. Madison would try to draw Henry into conversation. She even asked about the tax reform initiative that was all over the headlines. Henry shared that he was involved in the discussions happening in the House of Lords, but beyond that he did not seem inclined to share nor to ask for her thoughts on the matter.

Some mornings, she ate alone. Those were the hardest of all. Henry often went riding in the mornings with Theodore. He might mention it the night before, but most of the time the empty chair across from her was the only notice she received.

During the day, she called on her parents and the handful of friends she had in the city. She would take long walks in the park that was just two blocks away from the mansion. She invited Eve to drink tea and chat in her perfectly manicured gardens. Madison thought that they had received a lot of invitations when she lived with her parents … she was stunned by the number that arrived daily since she had become a marchioness.

In the late afternoon as she took her tea, she opened every missive and selected the ones for the next days and weeks which looked most interesting. This was her favorite part of the day. Well, her second favorite.

As the afternoon faded into evening, Henry would arrive home. To his credit, he was always ready for anything with a smile and a laugh. They would change into evening attire and then foray out to whatever social engagement Madison had selected from their piles and piles of invitations.

The best part of Madison's day was the time spent with Henry. He held her hand in the carriage as they rode to the home of another *ton* socialite. He danced with her, laughed with her, snuck kisses and intimate touches in shadowed corners. When they were alone in their bedrooms, he made love to her like it was the end of the world.

And once her eyes drifted closed in sleep, he returned to his rooms and Madison was alone again.

It was not the being alone that Madison minded. She made friends easily and did actually enjoy socializing. It was why she spent so much time looking through the invitations that arrived each day. She knew that as the Marchioness of Clydon, her attendance could confer status and importance on an event. So, she chose carefully. She attended intimate soirees given by less affluent members of the ton to help elevate their status. She avoided attending the galas of known gossips.

But the superficial nature of their relationship was starting to grind away at Madison's happiness. It was as if Henry was holding her at arm's length. He was happy to hold her on his arm while they paraded through the London Season. He was passionately attracted to her. But the details of his life, his passions and quirks, the issues that bothered him and fascinated him between the hours of ten in the morning and seven in the evening – those he seemed determined to keep to himself.

By the time two full weeks of this routine had passed, Madison had moved from confused to sad to outright frustrated and annoyed. And her handsome, charming husband continued on as if nothing was amiss.

Henry heard the toll of the grandfather clock at the end of the hallway just as his valet was finishing adjusting his tailcoat. Thanking the man, he headed for the doorway that connected his rooms to Madison's. He had not seen Madison since breakfast that morning. He'd sent along a note telling her what time to be ready for the evening's entertainment. He knocked on the door to her sitting room but opened it without waiting for a response.

Madison was seated at her dressing table. The maid was adding a bejeweled pin to the twisted plait at the nape of her neck. He could see her face reflected in the mirror. She did not immediately smile;

her face looked rather unhappy. She did not like having her hair fiddled with, he reminded himself.

"I see you received my note," Henry said, coming to stand beside her. Madison kept her eyes trained forward while the maid finished adding a few more pins and a necklace to her ensemble, but she did nod and offer a small smile. "Every time I see you, I think you get more beautiful," Henry said honestly, looking her over appreciatively.

Although she was thoroughly annoyed by it, Madison could not help the flutter of desire the flitted through her as Henry's eyes roved over her. She did not understand her husband at all; he made passionate love to her at night. He was attentive, complimentary, funny, at every *ton* social gathering they attended. But beyond that, their interactions were minimal. She did not see him at all during the day. Occasionally in the past week, they had passed a meal together. As much as she enjoyed their intimate encounters, Madison was beginning to feel the strain.

She cleared her throat and tried to push down the twin fires of annoyance and attraction. "Where are we going?" Madison asked. "Your note did not say. Only that I should dress formally. I assume this will do?" She motioned down at her gown. She had picked an outfit to match her mood: a dark gray, satin dress trimmed with black velvet ribbon. It almost looked like a mourning gown; that might even have been what her mother intended when she included it in her trousseau. It would certainly arouse comment from the other ladies they might see tonight. But as usual, Madison did not bother to spare a thought for the opinions of society gossips.

"You are perfect," Henry said, his gaze admiring. He noted the dark color of her gown but found it so striking against her bright golden blonde hair and alabaster skin that no thoughts of impropriety even entered his mind.

Letting her annoyance get the better of her, Madison snapped her fingers in front of Henry's face to get his attention back. Henry frowned. "Where are we going?" Madison asked again.

Henry deftly caught her outstretched hand, nipping at her wrist playfully. Madison's face must have betrayed the sparks that were raging inside of her because a self-satisfied smile bloomed on Henry's face. "I thought perhaps we would give the opera another try."

Madison leaned forward and looked out the window. "The weather does look more promising," she observed.

"And this time I have you all to myself." He slid his hand up her arm as he said it. Madison felt a little shiver of anticipation.

The theater slowly darkened around them as candles were snuffed and the assembled crowd shifted their focus to the stage. Madison leaned forward, eagerly listening as the overture began. In the darkness, Henry could only see her silhouette: he studied the sweep of her eyelashes, the delicate tip of her nose, the rounded curve of her bosom.

He could not resist the urge to touch her. He reached over and laid his hand casually atop her shoulder. She turned her head slightly, glancing at him, but then redirected her attention back to the stage. Slowly, softly, he began to stroke the bare skin from the top of her shoulder to the nape of her neck. Over and over again, until it was warm beneath his fingers. Madison continued to watch the stage.

Henry moved his hand lower. This time he did not use his fingertips. He slid his entire palm purposefully downward, beneath the neckline of her gown. He felt her sharp intake of breath as he cupped her breast. Slowly he began to massage it, feeling the rounded weight of her breast in his hand. He flicked a fingernail over her nipple. Madison bit her lip.

Her breath was coming heavier now. Henry continued his slow and deliberate exploration of her breasts. He even turned to watch the performance. When he finally withdrew his hand, her sigh was so deep he felt it. He moved his hand to her leg, and she caught it with her own, squeezing it hard.

But he was not done.

Henry moved his hand from her upper thigh, down towards her knee. Then in one smooth motion, he leaned forward as if he was picking something up off the ground. But when he sat up, he artfully slid his hand inside her skirt, up past her calf so that his fingertips were teasing the sensitive skin of her inner thigh. Madison did not make any pretense of looking at the stage. She turned to him, eyes wide, reflecting the light from below. Henry met her eyes, but he did not concede to her alarmed look.

Instead, he slid his fingers towards her hot center. Madison's mouth dropped open as his hand found her tender flesh. But she did not look away. She kept her eyes locked on his as he slowly caressed her, stroking gently. He could feel her wet desire building; his was too. But only one of them could be satisfied here and now, and Henry did not relent. He watched her eyes, felt her body beginning to tense. She reached out and grabbed the polished wooden banister of the box, gripping it hard.

Henry felt her body tighten and then release. He watched the waves of pleasure wash over her face, seeing the way she furrowed her brow and then bit her lip to keep from crying out in satisfaction.

Slowly, Madison's heart rate began to return to normal. She released the banister, but her chest continued to heave up and down with deep breaths. Henry slowly withdrew his hands, leaning back in his seat. He was surprised to find himself out of breath as well. He was as wound up with desire as she was.

They sat still as statues for the remainder of the performance, their bodies pressed close together in the dark of their private box.

As the final notes of the performance floated over the audience, Madison leaned over and whispered huskily into Henry's ear: "This is the second opera I have attended and the second I have barely watched."

"Are you complaining?" He asked, a dark eyebrow raised.

Madison leaned forward and kissed him on the mouth as the room slowly came back to light around them. Henry took that as his answer.

As she drew back from the embrace, Madison was aware that several pairs of eyes were watching them. Their opera box provided not just an excellent view of the stage, but put the occupants on display to the wider audience. And the newly christened Marchioness of Clydon was already a subject of intense interest.

Henry observed Madison closely, wondering how she would react to being caught in an intimate moment by so many prying eyes. But she seemed unbothered. She did not even glance at the patrons below or in the nearby boxes. She simply stood and offered him her hand so that he could guide her out.

As they emerged from the curtained confines of their box, the concourse was already busy with well-dressed opera-goers. Henry was perfectly content to walk past all of them and make their way downstairs towards their carriage, but Madison headed in the opposite direction. "Viscountess Herrin, what an unexpected pleasure!"

The middle-aged lady stood with her husband and two daughters. Henry could not help feeling slightly embarrassed. Viscountess Herrin had made her interest in him as a match for her elder daughter, Harriet, extremely obvious earlier in the season. But Madison did not seem bothered; she smiled widely and grasped Harriet's hand familiarly.

"Lady Warsham," Viscountess Herrin curtsied, addressing Madison by her new title. To her credit, the words did not stick in her throat. "Your gown is quite striking. All eyes were on you this evening."

Ignoring the dual implications of social impropriety, Madison smiled brightly. "You are so kind. I must say, being a wife has its privileges. I was not sad to bid adieu to the timid color palette of a debutante. I've always found richer hues more to my liking. Not all of us look as lovely in lavender as sweet Harriet here."

Harriet pinkened, but the rosy flush and accompanying smile did much for her delicate features. Henry spoke next: "Viscount Herrin, we have not had a chance to discuss your position on the issue of repealing the income tax. Perhaps you and your family would join us for tea tomorrow afternoon, and we can take the opportunity to discuss it further."

The Viscount nodded, opening his mouth to speak, but his wife cut him off. "Of course, Lord Warsham! We would be honored to join you and your new marchioness for tea tomorrow!" She exclaimed loudly. Several people nearby looked over at them.

Madison smiled graciously, but leaned closer to Harriet and said more quietly: "I would love to hear about your suitors so far this Season, Harriet. Now that I am married, you must allow me to chaperone and support you."

Harriet returned Madison's open-hearted smile. "I would be most honored, Lady Warsham," she said politely.

"Oh, enough of that," Madison said with a broad chuckle. "You and I will always be Madison and Harriet to each other, I hope."

"Of course," Harriet agreed.

Henry slid his arm around his wife's waist as he turned and spoke further to Viscount Herrin. After a few minutes, he felt the squeeze of Madison's hand. He understood immediately. "Thank you for the conversation. You must excuse us, it has been a busy day. We look forward to seeing you all tomorrow." They exchanged a few more pleasant nothings with the family, and then Henry turned and led Madison towards the stairs. This time she followed.

"That was very well done," Henry commented as they descended the stairs to the ground floor of the theatre.

"I have felt a bit guilty about snapping you up from under Harriet's nose. I know she was quite taken with you," Madison said honestly. "Do you remember the first night we met? You were speaking with her —"

"I remember perfectly." Henry tried not to smirk. "You inserted yourself quite deftly."

"It is a talent of mine."

"I have learned," he said with an indulgent smile. "The Viscountess looked quite pleased by the time we departed. Your attention to her daughter will not go unnoticed."

"Nor will your invitation to an intimate, exclusive tea," Madison countered. "It was all well done, I think. What is the good of a lofty title if we do not use it to help others?"

"I have never really thought of it quite that way," Henry admitted.

Madison sighed as they stepped outside. Sometimes it was so easy between them, she could almost forget the unhappiness she felt the rest of the time. Henry seemed to read her so well, understanding her social maneuvers and lending his help without even having to be asked. But he was woefully oblivious to the hurt she felt each night when he slipped from her bed, or in the morning when he left the house without a word of inquiry into her day. Perhaps she should say something to him … express how different this marriage was than she had envisioned. Henry had never said an unkind word to her. Surely, he would be responsive?

But Madison felt her pride stepping clearly into her pathway. She should not have to beg for his love and attention. Besides, if she had to ask for it, if she felt like a burden or a task to be checked off his list … it would not be the same. She wanted his love, but only if it was freely given.

As they climbed into their carriage, she felt very much alone at a crossroads.

Chapter 15

"How do you like your rooms?" Erica asked excitedly. "I watched as they were redecorating them. The colors you chose are completely different from how mother had it. It was such fun to watch the transformation."

"They are very ornate, just like the rest of the house," Madison responded.

Erica laughed. "Yes, it's a bit of a monstrosity, isn't it?"

"It is lavish," Madison said, but she did smile a little. The mansion she now lived in was a kind of monster, though not one she was scared of. There were so few like it in London, where most well-to-do families occupied luxurious but much smaller townhouses, that it was the constant subject of interest to people Madison met. Perhaps behemoth would be a better word, she mused to herself.

They were at a garden party. Denise had announced it would be their last social engagement before she and Erica returned to their families, waiting for them at home outside of London. Madison had for the most part enjoyed getting to know Henry's sisters. Especially Erica, who was closer to her in age and temperament.

Because this was a daytime attraction, Henry was nowhere to be seen. While at first Madison had tried not to take his absentee lifestyle personally, chalking it up to his arcane views of an ideal marriage, his absence was beginning to chafe more and more with each passing day. She knew the work he did as a member of the House of Lords was extremely important to him; not because he had told her, but because it was so often the explanation he gave for his absences and activities. Although he knew that she read the news sheets, and had often commented on her cleverness and wit, he had never once attempted to discuss it with her. She was reminded of the exchange she had witnessed between her parents a few weeks ago, when they discussed the business issues sent by the steward back at Sommerfield. She could recall many instances where her parents talked together about what was best to be done for the wellbeing of the estate or related business interests. Yet, Henry seemed entirely content with confining their relationship to the topical and physical. Was her only value to Henry as a social ornament and bedroom partner?

Although it was getting later on in the spring, the air had a definite chill and Madison found herself rubbing her arms up and down to generate what warmth she could. Erica was talking into her ear, but what Madison saw from across the garden shocked her so much, she did not hear a word her sister-in-law said.

Weaving his way through the crowd, clearly having spotted her, was the one person that Madison could have least expected to see – beyond her own husband.

"Christopher!" Madison put her hands on her hips, staring at the man in astonishment as he came to stand before her.

"Hello to you too, Madison," he said sarcastically. He leaned forward and touched his cheek to hers by way of greeting. Erica's eyebrows flew up in surprise at their causal manner with each other.

"What are you doing here?" Madison asked, completely oblivious to her companion's surprise. She was still reeling from her own. "You are supposed to be in Spain. Did something happen?"

Christopher shrugged nonchalantly. "The business manager I sent ahead of me had most of the arrangements finalized before I even arrived. All I had to do was sign some paperwork and I was off. I did not feel the need to linger; Spain is too hot for my taste."

"I see." Madison could feel the frown on her face. She felt like a terrible friend; she had not spared Christopher a thought since his departure. And now he was home and about to get some news he was not going to be pleased to hear. "Christopher, I have something I need to tell you …" She began, breathing in awkwardly through her teeth.

"Lady Warsham, perhaps you could introduce me to your friend?" Erica chimed in, noting Madison's obvious discomfort.

"Lady Warsham?" Christopher repeated, looking slowly from Madison to Erica.

Madison cleared her throat. "This is my dear friend, Christopher Bowden, younger brother of

Viscount Bayfield. He is a childhood friend. Christopher, this is my sister-in-law, Lady Erica –"

"You are married?" Christopher let out an incredulous laugh. "Madison, you really did not waste any time –"

"Christopher," she said in a warning tone. "I do not want you –"

"Lady Warsham …" Christopher paused as realization dawned on his face. Madison wrinkled her nose, knowing what was coming. "Madison, you didn't …"

Madison turned to her sister-in-law. "Erica, would you excuse us for just a moment? We need to speak about some sensitive family matters."

Erica looked from Madison to Christopher and back again, a worried expression on her face. But she nodded. "I will be with Denise. If you need us."

Madison watched her depart, waiting until she was several yards away before turning back to Christopher.

"Have you lost your mind?" Christopher said, arms crossed as he looked down at her.

"Excuse me?" Her hands were back on her hips, but now the look on her face was disdain rather than surprise.

"You married him? The one man I told you to steer clear of?" Christopher was shaking his head in disbelief.

"You did not tell me to –"

"I implied it! I told you I did not like the man."

Madison was well and truly angry now. "Excuse me if I do not live and die by your judgments. You are not exactly known for making good ones yourself," she said, seething.

His eyes narrowed. "Where is this sainted husband of yours? I have not seen him yet this afternoon."

"He's not here," she said through gritted teeth.

"Trouble in paradise already, Madison?"

"As a matter of fact, there is," she bit out.

"I cannot pretend to be surprised. You were so caught up in making a love match that you fell for the first man who took a shine to you." Christopher's words burned.

"You are a terrible friend," she said angrily. She wanted to hurl a whole slew of expletives at him, but people were starting to stare. So instead she turned and walked away. Erica appeared at her side, looking nervous. She opened her mouth to speak, but Madison shook her head. "I'm sorry, Erica. But I need to leave now."

Henry climbed the stairs from the great hall two at a time. He was looking forward to seeing his wife. Much to his surprise, months into knowing her, weeks into marriage, she maintained a persistent hold on his mind. He had attended more *ton* social events since meeting Madison than he ever had before. But with Madison at his side, they did not seem so tedious. It seemed the more time he spent with her, the more fascinating and attractive he found her.

It was becoming more and more difficult to go about his daily routines. As he discussed the upcoming parliamentary vote with Theodore, he found himself wondering what Madison's thoughts would be. While he examined the updated accounts his estate manager had sent from Carcliffe Castle, he pictured taking Madison there for the first time and showing her around the historic estate. This was not how he had pictured marriage. It was certainly not what he had observed in his own parents' union. The whole situation was damn disconcerting.

Out of habit, he went to his rooms first. He shrugged off his burgundy tailcoat and then began unbuttoning the matching silk waistcoat. It was quite late. Madison was surely already abed. Even if she attended a late-night event, such as a ball, he had noticed that she rarely stayed out past midnight. While many *ton* socialites would be dancing into the wee hours of the morn, Madison could reliably be found curled up in bed by that time, warm and inviting.

Sitting down on the edge of the bed to remove his boots, a folded paper on the dressing table caught his eye. As he crossed the room, he recognized Madison's handwriting on the outside of the note. It was folded in half and propped up so it stood like a tent on the polished wood surface of the dressing table, next to a selection of cuff links and combs. He picked it up and flicked open the paper with the tip of his finger.

Henry –

I have a terrible headache this evening.

I think it would be best if we kept our own rooms tonight.

-Madison

He reread the note several times. When he looked up, he found himself staring through the open door of his bedroom, into the sitting room, at the closed door that led to Madison's apartments.

It was a completely reasonable request ... to be left alone when one was feeling unwell. He mulled it over for a second, then decided. Henry walked determinedly towards her door. He would honor her wishes, of course, but first he wanted to assure himself that she was alright. He lifted his hand to open the door, but then stopped, realizing the note was still clutched in his hand. Slowly, he uncrumpled the paper and held it up so he could see it in the firelight. He read it again.

She wanted to be alone. He sighed as he turned away from her door and walked back to his room. He placed the note back on the dressing table and continued undressing. As he pulled off his shirt and laid down in his bed alone, Henry could not shake the feeling that something more was going on with his wife.

Chapter 16

When Denise and Erica stopped at the house the next morning to say their farewells, Madison was still in a foul mood. She had spent a fitful night alone in bed, tossing and turning and not sleeping. At one point, she had even considered giving up her pretense of a headache and going to join Henry in his bed, just for the sake of a distraction. But she had dismissed that idea with an angry *smack* of her pillow.

Damn Christopher and his self-centered notions. *Damn* Henry and the nonstop game he was playing with her heart.

The most infuriating part was that she was afraid Christopher was right. Maybe she had been so hell-bent on a fairytale happy ending that she had gotten married too soon. She had undoubtedly fallen for the first man who held her interest. She had gotten married on the belief that the love between her and Henry just needed time to grow and flower. Their physical relationship may be flourishing, but their emotional one … not so much.

Her irritation spilled over as her maid was attempting to fix her hair. "Oh, just let it be!" She cried testily, shaking the maid's hands free of her head. The maid looked stricken.

"I am sorry, my lady, if you would prefer –"

"I would prefer to be left alone," Madison bit out.

The poor young woman bobbed a curtsey and retreated as fast as she could. Madison cringed when she heard the door close hard. There was no excuse for her behavior. She sighed and picked up the brush, pulling it through her hair in long strokes. She would need to go find the maid as soon as she was dressed and apologize.

She looked in the mirror, considered plaiting her hair for about half a second, and then decided she did not have the desire nor the motivation. Untying her dressing gown, she walked over to the bed, where the maid had laid out a soft muslin day dress printed with small blue flowers. Madison started to dress only to realize that she would need help fastening the buttons at the back. Resigning herself to ringing the bell for the maid and begging forgiveness, she was startled by the knock on her door. Not the door to the hallway, but the one that connected her rooms to Henry's.

"Yes?" Madison called, trying to keep her voice steady.

Henry opened the door slowly. When he saw her standing by the edge of the bed he offered a tentative smile. "How are you feeling this morning?" He asked.

"Well enough," she answered. Henry stepped into the room.

"I am glad to hear it," he said. He joined his hands behind his back, looking awkward. "Denise and Erica are here to say their goodbyes. I can tell them you are not feeling up to it if you would prefer to remain here …"

"No, no," Madison shook her head. "Of course, I will see them off." She started to move towards the door, then remembered her predicament. "I dismissed my maid a bit prematurely. Could you help me fasten my gown?"

Henry's smile grew as he crossed the room obligingly. Standing behind her, he began to fasten the long line of delicate mother-of-pearl buttons that reached from the small of her back to the nape of her neck. He could not resist running a finger up the triangle of exposed skin. Before he fastened the last few buttons, he leaned down and pressed a kiss between her shoulder blades. He felt her shiver.

Madison bit her lip to capture the little moan that tried to escape. Every time she was in his arms she felt her resolve start to crumble. It was impossible to think clearly with his lips pressed against her. She felt her eyes flutter closed as the heat started to build deep within her … but the distant neigh of a horse brought her back to earth. Denise and Erica waited below. She cleared her throat and stepped away from Henry, smoothing the arms of her gown and adjusting the neckline.

"Shall we go down?" She asked, already headed for the door.

Henry followed her out into the hallway, intending to take her arm and escort her down the stairs. But Madison was already on her way down the staircase into the entry hall, her feet moving inordinately fast over the carpeted steps. She did not spare him so much as a glance over her shoulder. In the pit of his stomach, Henry felt something uncomfortable begin to take hold.

"Good morning," Madison said brightly, embracing each of Henry's sisters and touching cheeks affectionately. Erica and Denise had waited in the entry hall, both garbed for travel in pelisses and hats. "Won't you come have a spot of tea with us before you head off?" Madison offered, motioning towards the open doors into the morning room.

Erica looked hopeful, but Denise shook her head. "No, thank you, dear. But we really must get on as soon as possible. If we're to make it to the halfway mark before nightfall, we haven't much time to lose."

"I am surprised you aren't determined to push straight through," Henry scoffed as he joined them in the entry hall.

"I insisted on the stop," Erica interjected, giving her brother and sister a wry smile.

"She also wanted to detour to visit Helen, but of course I shut that down immediately," Denise said, accepting the kiss that Henry pressed to her cheek.

"Helen is one of your other sisters, yes?" Madison asked though she was fairly certain already.

"Yes, she's the next eldest to me," Erica confirmed. "And I am sure she is just dying for an update on the situation here in London," she added with a conspiratorial smile.

"I look forward to meeting her soon," Madison said politely, struggling to keep up a cheery demeanor. Erica looked away awkwardly. Denise glanced over at her new sister-in-law with interest. Erica had recounted something of the garden party exchange the day before, but Denise would not betray that confidence.

"Perhaps we can gather at Carcliffe Castle in the fall," Erica suggested, looking to Henry.

"Perhaps," he conceded, rolling his eyes and throwing Madison a look of exasperation.

"Best we are off," Denise said, clearly tired of the idle chatter. She embraced her brother, while Erica and Madison pulled each other into a tight hug of farewell.

"How is it going, with your new marchioness? Truly?" Denise asked her brother quietly.

Henry frowned. "Everything is going perfectly," he said, his eyes narrowing. "What makes you think otherwise?"

This time Denise rolled her eyes. She gave her brother's hands a tight squeeze. "You need to pay more attention," she said cryptically. Before Henry could ask what she meant, Denise had stepped away to bid adieu to Madison.

Denise kissed each of Madison's cheeks and held her hands tightly in her own. "Chin up, Maddie," she said with a smile. "You are the Marchioness now. And whatever the rest of the world thinks, it is my personal opinion that the lady is almost always cleverer than the lord. It will probably be up to you to figure things out and then educate my little brother." On that ominous note, she stepped away, taking Erica's hand and pulling her out the door.

Henry followed his sisters outside, helping them into their carriage and waving as they disappeared out of the courtyard. Madison drifted into the morning room, moving aimlessly between the damask upholstered furniture. It was a beautiful room, decorated in yellow, gold, and ivory. The windows were positioned to catch the morning light, and with the spring sunshine pouring in through the glass panes the room positively glowed.

When Henry came back inside, he found her standing in a pool of light, the sun shimmering around her like a halo. She took his breath away. For a moment, he had no thoughts in his head, no words to say, no jokes to make. He was just stunned by her ethereal beauty.

"I will miss them," Madison said with a sigh. "It's a pity they live so far away."

"Far from London, yes. But Erica and Helen are relatively close to Carcliffe Castle. Once we adjourn to the country at the end of the Season, you can see them as much as you wish. More than I wish, most likely," he said with an impish smile.

Madison did not laugh, or even smile. She sighed again and turned away.

"Are you alright? You are sure your headache isn't lingering?" Henry approached her, taking her hand in his. He caught her chin with his finger and tipped it up so he could see her face clearly.

She met his gaze directly. She looked … sad. Staring down at her, his look implored her to open up to him. Madison sighed again. "I've quarreled with a friend and it is weighing heavy on my mind. That is all." With that excuse, she stepped away.

She turned towards an arrangement of flowers sitting on the table next to the sofa and busied her hands with re-arranging them. One by one, she pulled out a few that were wilting, laying them on the marble table-top. She delicately plucked aside a few petals edged with brown, adding them to her little pile.

"I have an audience with the Duke of Firth this morning to discuss the tax repeal and plan our next steps, but I have a bit of time now. Is there anything I can do to help?" He offered.

Madison rolled her eyes. Of course, he had no plans to linger. "Your help is the last thing I need in this particular endeavor," she said under her breath.

Henry's handsomely arched dark brown eyebrows shot up. "Pardon me?" He said, thinking he must have misheard her.

"I –" as she spoke she yanked another stem from the arrangement in front of her. The leaves caught on the stems around them and the whole vase toppled over. Madison reached to try and catch it, but it crashed to the ground with a mighty *crack*, sending flowers, water, and shards of porcelain across the floor. "Oh, now look what you've done!" Madison cried, falling to her knees and reaching for the mess.

"What I've done?" Henry echoed, completely confused.

"I've quarreled with Christopher, I've been unforgivably rude to the maid, now I'm breaking things," she rambled in exasperation as she gathered up the flowers.

"Christopher? Christopher … Bowden?" Henry said, puzzled, as he leaned down and started collecting the shards of porcelain from the wet floor. "I thought you were talking about Eve."

"Eve is not my only friend." She rolled her eyes again, no longer bothering to rein in her irritation.

"Of course not, I –"

"I have known Christopher for a decade. Much longer than Eve. He's the closest friend I have." Madison said stubbornly.

"I am not surprised you've quarreled; Christopher Bowden is one of the most disagreeable men I have ever met." Henry deposited the last shard of porcelain onto the table, where it could easily be swept into a waste bin, and stood up.

"I won't hear you speak against him." Madison also came to her feet, her knuckles white as they clutched the spray of dripping wet flowers.

"I did not speak against him," Henry protested.

"You called him disagreeable!"

"That is just a statement of fact!"

Madison huffed in anger, stomping away from him to ring the bell for a maid to help with the rest of the cleanup. Henry shook his head, his eyes darting around the room as if he would somewhere there be able to find answers to the dozens of confusing questions roiling through him. His wife stood with her arms crossed, glaring at the room in general.

"I am going now," Henry said warily, taking a cautious step towards the door.

"Oh yes, off with you. I am sure you have very important business to attend to," Madison said fiercely, not looking at him.

He opened his mouth to say something but thought better of it. Whatever the words were that would make this situation better, he did not have them. He walked out the door without further comment, completely shocked by what had transpired between them.

Chapter 17

*H*enry entered his gentleman's club on Pall Mall with a mind weighed down by too many questions and too few answers. He did not acknowledge the steward who greeted him, barely even conscious of the man's presence. He wandered past the smoking room, with its heavy leather-upholstered chairs. Even though it was just past noon, there were several card games already in progress, but he passed those by as well. He found Theodore seated with another gentleman over two half-full snifters of brandy.

Theodore glanced over the other man's shoulder at his friend, and very subtly inclined his head towards the chair next to him, inviting Henry to join them. Henry shook his head mutedly and instead retreated to a sofa on the other side of the room. He ordered tea from the liveried young man who was seeing to the members' needs and settled in to wait.

Throughout his meeting with the Duke of Firth, his mind had turned persistently back to his argument with Madison. He was becoming more and more convinced that the income tax repeal would negatively impact more people than it would help, and was trying to explain to the Duke how he had come to that conclusion. But whenever the Duke asked him a question, Henry found himself at a loss. He kept hearing echoes of his and Madison's argument from that morning. It was like a puzzle that he could not fit together.

For the life of him, he could not figure out how his sweet, amenable fiancée had transformed into such an unhappy wife. He cared deeply for Madison, a fact that was as surprising as it was unsettling to him. Henry was shocked to find that he preferred her company to almost everyone else's, and not just for the physical aspects. While he had expected a comfortable companionship, perhaps even friendship, what he had not expected was his emotional attachment to her. Nor her emotional volatility.

"You look like someone has shot your horse," Theodore said, appearing at his friend's side. The man he had been talking to was engaged in another conversation and headed out the door. Theodore poured himself a cup of tea from the pot that sat next to Henry and then tipped what remained of his snifter of brandy into the teacup. He held up the glass to Henry, silently offering to fortify his cup of tea as well, but Henry shook his head.

"The feeling would undoubtedly be similar," Henry said morosely. Theodore took a seat at the other end of the sofa, leaning back and propping one booted heel on his opposite knee.

"Why do I assume this has something to do with your newly acquired state of matrimony?" Theodore asked, his face grim.

"Because you have nothing positive to say about the aforementioned state," Henry said, his voice a bit sharp. But then he sighed because, of course, his friend was right. "I thought it was going well at first. The wedding day … and night …" he paused. Theodore raised his eyebrows, but Henry did not elaborate. "Suffice it to say, things were well on all fronts at the beginning."

"But now they are not."

"Now they are not."

They sat in silence for a few moments, both men staring out on the room of *ton* gentlemen quietly going about their afternoon entertainments.

"I had imagined that once we were married, Madison and I would settle into a kind of quiet companionship, much like my parents shared. They were pleasant enough to each other, appeared at meals and social events. But essentially, they were their own people, with their own lives," Henry mused.

"That sounds significantly better than what I saw," Theodore said, his voice carefully controlled to be even and flat. Henry did not respond to that; he did not want to stir up his friend's ghosts.

"If I am perfectly honest with myself, I do not think that I ever saw my mother and father exchange anything beyond the paltriest of pleasantries. I do not even think they were friends, per se, because I do not recall them having any common interests," Henry continued.

Theodore opened his mouth to respond, but then closed it. Henry wanted to ask what he was going to say, but the fact that Theodore had thought better of it dissuaded him from pressing him.

Henry sipped his tea, regretting his refusal of brandy to stiffen the drink. He drained away the last of the warm, comforting liquid. "They died when I was a teenager, but thanks to my sisters I have been lucky to be spared most of the pains of their absence. I do wish they were alive now so that I could talk to them," Henry admitted quietly.

Next to him, Theo made a deep, masculine sound in his throat. "I wish I could help you, my friend. But on this account, I do not have any advice to offer," Theo said gruffly.

The two friends sat there for a long time, not talking. Their dark aspects kept the other club patrons from approaching them. As the afternoon faded into evening, they each engaged in deep debate with their personal demons.

Madison had spent another night alone in her bed. She did not need to leave a note for Henry this time; he stayed away all on his own. Madison wasn't sure if she was disappointed by that or relieved by it. If Henry had come to her while she slept, slid beneath the coverlet, and wrapped his body around hers, would she have refused him? She knew the answer. She would have welcomed him, would have drowned herself in his kisses and caresses, and ignored the pain that gripped her heart.

When the sun rose, so did she. She rang for her maid, knowing it was earlier than the poor girl would be expecting but also knowing there was nothing to be done for it. She carefully selected a favorite dress from her trousseau: a rich, autumnal gold muslin gown that complemented her eyes. She chose it not because of how it looked, but how it made her feel. It was casual, the type of dress she would only wear at home or with family; made for the country rather than the glittering spectacle of a London season. But it symbolized everything she hoped for between herself and her husband: honesty, softness, warmth. The stripping away of the bedazzled, formal armor of balls and parties. This morning, she wanted Henry to see *her*. Not the marchioness, not the belle of every society ball. Just her, his wife.

Then she made her way downstairs, called for breakfast and tea, and sat down with the stack of newspapers to wait for her husband.

"Madison!" Henry said, coming to an unsteady stop in the doorway. He was startled to find her already seated at the formal dining table. Taking a deep breath, he walked slowly around the table to his seat at the head. "You are not usually awake this early," he said cautiously.

Madison nodded in acknowledgment. "There is something important I needed to discuss with you, and I wanted to make sure we would have time before any of your morning engagements," she said matter-of-factly.

Henry poured his tea and sat down. "Alright," he said, bracing himself for whatever was coming next.

Very calmly, Madison put her news sheet aside, set down her cup of tea, and turned to face Henry.

"Do you love me?"

Henry leaned back in his chair like he had been dealt a physical blow. He had just enough presence of mind to set down his cup of tea before he spilled it all over his lap. "What?"

Seemingly unaffected by his obvious discomfiture, Madison repeated her question coolly: "Do you love me?"

An awkward little laugh escaped from Henry's mouth, and Madison's composure cracked. Henry saw her bite her lip; her frustration was building. He had no idea what to say but he started to speak anyway: "Madison, I –"

"Fine. At least now I know." She took the cloth napkin that had rested in her lap and tossed it on the table.

"That's not fair. You caught me completely off guard." Henry reached for her hand. He was surprised when she did not resist.

Feeling the warmth of his hand, the physical connection that was so strong between them giving her strength, Madison squeezed his hand. She leaned forward, her gold-green eyes shining with emotion, looking right into his. Henry felt like she was trying to see into his soul. But if he did not know what was there, how could she?

"Did I?" She asked more softly.

"Yes," Henry said, hearing the pleading in his voice. "You do not know what you're asking –"

"Henry, I know exactly what I am asking." Unable to hold his gaze, she glanced away. The pain rippling through her was real and physical. Henry could see it in every line of her tense body. But somehow, she found the strength to turn back to him. "All I ever wanted was a true marriage. A love match, like my parents."

"A true marriage? What does that even mean, Madison?" Henry felt his own frustration rising. He had already given her so much more than he had anticipated when they first met. He was infatuated with her. Why couldn't that be enough?

"It means love, Henry! It means sharing our lives with one another!" Her grip on his hand was tightening but neither of them pulled away.

"We do share our lives! We sit here and eat breakfast each morning, we attend balls and soirees and share a bed. What does love have to do with it?"

"Love has everything to do with it!" Madison argued. She could feel herself bordering on hysteria but could do nothing to contain her emotions. "And we do not share our lives, Henry. You spend your time in meetings, or closeted in your study, or at the club, or riding with Theodore. I do not know anything about what occupies your mind, what worries you, where you find fulfillment. Despite all of my attempts, you will not let me in. We do not even sleep in the same bed!"

Henry shook his head, unable to process what he was hearing. "You want me to tell you about my meetings, and to sleep with you instead of returning to my own rooms …" he repeated, trying to make sense of things.

Madison rolled her eyes, awed by his thick-headedness. "Before you were married, you said you admired my mind and my cleverness. You said you enjoyed spending time with me. And yet, most of the time I am alone in this cavernous mansion."

"I do enjoy spending time with you. I have done more socializing in the past two months than in the last two years. Do you think that has to do with the riveting conversational prowess of our hosts?" Henry asked sarcastically. He moved to cross his arms and realized their hands were still clasped: a desperate connection even as angry words flew between them.

Madison seemed to realize it too. She stared down at their hands, studying the way that her smaller fingers intertwined with his long, strong ones. She felt the way her smooth skin rubbed against his rougher palms, calloused from holding the reins of his horse. They were such different people, she was beginning to realize. But yet here they sat, their hands and lives inextricably intertwined.

"Stay with me," she said quietly.

"What?" Henry leaned forward to hear her better.

She looked up from their hands, meeting his gaze again. The shining in her eyes had given way to tears; she was just holding them back. "Let's spend the day together, just the two of us. We can stay here, we can even go riding in the park, let's just be together." Even as she made the offer, she sincerely hoped he did not want her to get on a horse and go for a ride.

"I have an engagement with Theo." Henry hated himself as the words left his mouth. He saw Madison's face crumple and the first two tears escape down her cheeks in parallel rivers. She pulled her hand free to wipe them from her cheeks.

"Well then," she said with a sharp exhalation of breath. She stood up, pushing in her chair neatly and smoothing the folds of her muslin gown. "Now I know," she said in an echo her words just minutes before. "For once, I am going to be the one who leaves."

Chapter 18

*A*lthough she was still boiling inside from her earlier encounter with Henry, Madison felt she was doing a good job covering her emotions and holding them at bay. After a good cry alone in her rooms, she emerged to find Henry gone.

Determined not to sit at home alone and stew in her misery, Madison accepted an invitation to an afternoon tea party that Eve was hosting. Lady Brockton had planned a large afternoon event. There were six tables beautifully arranged in her conservatory with fresh-cut flowers and intricately patterned chintz tea sets. At each table, four ladies were seated according to a formal seating arrangement expertly prepared by Eve to balance mutual acquaintances and interests. *She really is growing into the role of a proper society hostess*, Madison thought to herself as she nibbled on a delicate teacake.

At Madison's left was Harriet, the daughter of Viscount and Viscountess Herrin. At her right was Lady Merrywright, one of the young women whom she and Henry had caught gossiping so unkindly about her at Countess Spencer's musicale. However, the young, newly married woman seemed genuinely determined to make amends and had been conversing kindly with Madison and Harriet. Across the table was another guest that Madison had met only in passing, a middle-aged woman known as Viscountess Crimpton. Madison could not recall her given name.

"I have not had a chance to attend yet. Was the performance as moving as everyone is saying?" Lady Merrywright asked as she poured some more cream into her tea.

"I thought so, yes. But I am not an expert in opera by any means," Harriet answered, tipping her head towards Madison: "Lady Warsham was there the same evening as me. What did you think?"

Despite the current state of her relationship with Henry, Madison could not help blushing at the memory of the opera. "I admit that I was a bit distracted that evening," Madison said, trying not to look too obvious.

Harriet seemed oblivious, but Lady Merrywright chuckled and winked at Madison conspiratorially. "It would be easy to be distracted by a husband as handsome as the Marquess," the married woman said knowingly.

"Indeed, the Marquess does seem to cause a stir wherever he goes," Viscountess Crimpton added from across the table.

Madison frowned. Something about the woman's tone stirred an uneasy feeling in the pit of her stomach. But she was not one to back down from such an obvious challenge. "Do tell us what you mean by that, Viscountess," Madison said pointedly, eyebrows raised.

Harriet looked worried, but the Viscountess smiled over the rim of her teacup. "My husband mentioned that the Marquess of Clydon was seen having tea with the Countess of Blyth and that it aroused some comment from the other visitors to the tearoom."

Already sensing she did not want to know the answers to the questions that started to propagate in her head, Madison reached for a scone and spread it with jam. She refused to look at the Viscountess, as if she could not even be bothered. "I am not acquainted with that particular lady," she said nonchalantly.

Lady Merrywright tried to change the subject. "Could you pass me a scone, Lady Warsham? Lady Brockton's cook has quite a reputation –"

But Viscountess Crimpton interrupted her. "You may not be, of course, as you are newly arrived in London. But the Marquess has been *very* well acquainted with the Countess for many years."

"I see," Madison said through gritted teeth.

"It seems that acquaintance has not faded, even as the handsome Marquess has found some temporary entertainment elsewhere," the Viscountess continued.

Madison thought she might scream. Lady Merrywright broke in bravely. "That is quite enough. I do not think that Viscountess Herrin would appreciate you subjecting her daughter to such talk. It is not appropriate or befitting a lady."

Viscountess Crimpton pursed her lips, surprised to be taken to task by the younger woman. She glanced around the table, and finding only frosty faces, stood up. "Do excuse me, ladies," she said, departing towards the other side of the room.

Madison sighed. She reached over and squeezed Lady Merrywright's hand gratefully. "You are a dear," she said sincerely. Looking over at Harriet, she apologized: "I am so sorry to leave you, I know I promised we could have a walk in the park later to catch up. But I find I need to return home."

"Of course, think nothing of it," Harriet said, her brow furrowed with worry. Madison stood up herself and started walking to the door. Eve caught up with her in the foyer.

"Are you alright?" Eve asked, touching her gloved arm gently.

Madison nodded, but then her chest heaved and she shook her head. Eve saw the way Madison's lower lip quivered. A true friend, Eve did not even glance over her shoulder to check on her other guests. She took Madison's arm and steered her across the foyer into the library. She closed the door behind them and then came to sit next to Madison, who had sunk dejectedly onto the chaise. Eve sat in silence, waiting until Madison was ready to speak.

"He has a mistress, Eve."

"Henry?" Eve said in disbelief.

"Viscountess Crimpton laid it out for me quite clearly." Madison gestured back towards the conservatory where the rest of the guests were still enjoying their tea.

"That woman is a busy body. Don't listen to her," Eve said, her arms crossed and her dislike evident. "People are jealous, Madison. You made the match of the Season! And it is clear to everyone that Henry is smitten with you. Now that you are the Marchioness, people are going to be hypercritical –"

"And I am just supposed to let it go?"

"You can rise above it. You have never let gossips bother you before."

"No one has gossiped about my husband's infidelity before."

"Please, Maddie, just talk to Henry."

She had tried that. For weeks, she had been talking and trying to draw her husband out. Trying to understand him and to help him understand her. But so far it had gotten her nothing but disappointment and now, humiliation.

"I am done talking to Henry. I need to find out for myself." Madison said, her voice hardening.

"I see now why you are not an early riser. When I decided to wait up for you, I did not expect to be here all night."

Christopher gritted his teeth at the unexpected voice ringing in his ears. Even in the darkened room, he knew the voice instantly. Long years of friendship. "No one asked you to wait."

"No, I was very careful not to let your staff know I was here. I did not want to alarm anyone." Madison leaned forward into the light spilling into Christopher's office from the hallway. She looked tired but determined.

"Heaven forbid you knock on the door like a normal person," Christopher observed. He returned briefly to the hall, bringing back a candle which he used to light two sconces on either side of the door.

Light spilled across the room, fully illuminating Madison. Her fists were clenched into balls at her sides as she sat in a wooden chair in the far corner of the room. "After our last conversation, I was not assured of my entrance."

Christopher said nothing.

"Despite that, I am here to ask for your help."

"Do you need an escort back to Sommerfield?"

Her eyes flashed. "I have decided to stop perseverating on your infuriating behavior and to forgive you. You can make it up to me by helping me."

He looked like he wanted to argue, but the determined lines of her face discouraged him. He sighed with resignation as he sank into a chair. "What is it?"

"I need an audience with the Countess of Blyth."

"So, go to her house and present your calling card. What do you need me for?"

Madison rolled her eyes. The golden-green orbs looked dangerous in the flickering candlelight. "It needs to be more discreet than that. She has a certain...*reputation*."

"Of that, I am aware," Christopher said drolly.

"Eww," Madison shivered, repulsed.

"We are not acquainted," Christopher assured her, though he was amused at her reaction.

"But she would consent to meet you, yes? You are her … type?" She said hesitantly.

"I am not sure if that is a compliment or an insult."

"I am," Madison said unequivocally, her nose wrinkled in disgust.

"You want me to arrange an audience with the Countess of Blyth, but not to tell her the audience is with you. I am assuming I will be the pretext for the meeting?" Christopher was starting to feel uneasy about this strange proposition.

"Exactly," Madison said with a decisive nod of her head. Her clenched fists had not relaxed.

"Dare I ask why?"

Madison frowned. She closed her eyes, trying to gather what remained of her pride and inner strength. "I believe she is Henry's mistress."

Though it took every measure of his self-control, Christopher did not make a snide comment. And Madison was thankful for it. But his face said it all, and Madison knew him well enough to read it. "Are you sure you want to do this, Madison?" He asked.

She nodded sadly. "Yes, I think I must."

Christopher sighed audibly but then nodded his head slowly. "Alright, I will do it."

Standing with her back against the wall, Madison watched Christopher leave through the doorway on the adjacent wall. That was their signal. Walking slowly enough not to call attention to herself, smiling and nodding, throwing in a little wave here and there, Madison weaved her way through the ballroom and into the hallway.

Christopher was a deductive master. After their conversation the previous night – or technically in the wee hours of the morning – he had returned to his gentleman's club to lay the requisite groundwork. He was a well-known ladies' man; they had agreed it would not be hard to build on that reputation. By midday, he had sent Madison a note saying that he had bantered and put out to several open-mouthed gentlemen of the *ton* that he was interested in getting to know the Countess of Blyth better. Meanwhile, a couple of strategic afternoon social calls had been all it took for Madison to figure out which party the well-known widow would most likely be attending this evening. Madison accepted her own invitation to the gala ball, and Christopher easily arranged for a note to be handed to the Countess upon her arrival asking her to meet him in the house's library.

Christopher was waiting outside the door of the library when Madison arrived. "Are you sure you do not want me to wait with you?" He asked, frowning.

"No, this is humiliating enough on my own," Madison said. "Thank you, Christopher," she said, feeling herself beginning to get emotional.

Christopher shook his head. "There's no time for that, Maddie. Best get inside, so I can make myself scarce." He opened the door and pushed her inside, disappearing down the hall himself just as the sound of footsteps on marble tiles began to echo from around the corner.

The woman that entered the room was tall. It was the first thing Madison noticed about her. *Of course,* she thought to herself. It took all her effort to beat back the images that sprang to her mind of this tall, buxom woman wrapped around Henry.

The Countess started in surprise. She froze with her hand still on the door, looking around the library curiously. "Pardon me, my lady. I appear to have gotten turned around…" she started to back out of the room.

"No!" Madison said loudly, bringing the other woman's gaze back to her quickly. "You have found the right place."

The Countess of Blyth cocked her head to the side, considering. "I am meant to meet Lord Bowden," she said, watching for Madison's reaction.

"Lord Bowden will not be joining us."

The woman nodded, clearly interested. She closed the door and walked to stand behind the sofa, looking questioningly at Madison. "It's a pity; Lord Bowden has always been an interesting fellow. Rather an enigma. But I am sure our paths will cross another time." She put one hand on her well-rounded hip, her voluptuous figure highlighted by a gown that could only have been pulled off by a widow. "Tell me, what am I doing here? Who are you?"

"I am the Marchioness of Clydon," Madison said clearly, willing strength into her voice.

A dark smile grew on the other woman's face. "Henry's little marchioness. I have heard about you. I suppose it was inevitable we were going to meet eventually."

"Was it? How are you acquainted with my husband, Countess?" Madison said. The anger in her gut was giving her strength and fuel. She had no concern about stumbling over her words now.

"Do call me Selena, my dear, your husband certainly does," the Countess said with a harsh smile.

"I do not much care what my husband calls you." Madison countered. Her fists were balled, her fingernails digging into her palms – the little pinpricks of pain helping her keep herself under control.

"Lying does not become you," Selena said. She ran her fingers sensually over the curved back of the sofa as she spoke. "I gather you care very much about my interactions with Henry. Otherwise, you would not have gone to the trouble of your little ruse to get me here." She used Henry's name casually and familiarly. Madison knew it was meant to needle her, but that did not stop it from having the desired effect.

Her heart hammered in her chest as she asked her next question: "When was the last time you saw my husband?"

"Last week."

The words hit Madison like bullets. But Selena was not done.

"I suppose we saw one another three or four times last month; it is hard to keep track. I know he was busy with the wedding. But now that his normal schedule has resumed, I expect we will resume our regular cadence." As Selena spoke, Madison felt each word hit her. Physical pain in her stomach, chest, and heart. Who knew heartbreak would feel so visceral?

But Madison was determined she would not break down in front of Henry's mistress. She may be humiliated in front of the entire *ton* – for surely Viscountess Crimpton was not the only one who knew of his private assignations – but she would not fall to pieces in front of this woman. She swallowed hard and stood up, keenly aware of the height differential. She came around the furniture to stand behind the sofa as well, only a few feet away from Selena.

"I have noted your information. You may go, *Countess,*" Madison said coldly.

Anger flared in the other woman's eyes; Selena did not appreciate being dismissed. But Madison outranked her, and any tangle between them would not reflect positively on the older, less popular woman. Selena decided to thrust in one last dagger.

"You should not blame him, my dear. Henry is a virile man. You cannot expect him to be satisfied with a little flower bud of a debutante when he has already tasted the bloom of experience." Selena turned for the door. But before she left, she glanced back over her shoulder and added: "Besides, a rake never truly changes his ways."

Madison didn't think. As the Countess of Blyth's footsteps faded away down the hall, she felt her composure start to unravel. She turned away and left the room. It was like the walls, rooms, and faces around her all blurred into something completely unintelligible. Somehow, she made it from the library outside to her carriage. But she had no memory of it. She kept hearing the same word over and over again in her head, flashing in bright red in her mind's eye: *rake, rake, rake*. The one thing she was most afraid of had happened: she was married to an unreformed rake.

Chapter 19

"When is Lady Warsham expected home?" Henry asked as he shrugged off his overcoat into the waiting arms of his butler.

The man gave him an odd look, but then answered: "Lady Warsham is upstairs, my lord."

Henry frowned. "Already? That seems unusually early to return from her usual evening engagements." He was beginning to feel uncomfortable echoes of the conversation he had with his butler upon arriving home only a few days ago.

The butler shook his head. "You misunderstand, my lord. Lady Warsham did not go out at all this evening."

"Again? Has she truly not left the house at all in the last two days?" Henry asked in disbelief. The butler nodded.

Henry's frown deepened. Madison might be upset with him, but one of the few things he did confidently know about her was that she loved socializing.

Dismissing the servants, he stood in the entry hall musing over his options. He could retire to his study. There was a decanter full of strong scotch whiskey waiting for him there. Or he could go upstairs and try to smooth things over with his wife. He looked around at the tall walls of the entry hall, ornately adorned with life-size portraits and lush landscapes. With a sigh, he made up his mind and started up the stairs.

When he knocked on the door to her room, he got no response. *Perhaps she was already in bed*, he thought to himself. He opened the door cautiously, finding her sitting room darkened. He fought the urge to give up and retreat to his rooms. The door to her bedroom stood ajar. Something in his gut told him that she was not asleep. Henry pushed open the door gently.

Madison was sitting up in bed, staring out the window. The curtains were wide open, letting in bright rays of moonlight. When she heard him come in she turned abruptly away from the window and back towards him. She did not look surprised to see him, but she did not speak.

Henry cleared his throat awkwardly. "The servants told me you did not go out this evening. Are you feeling unwell?"

"Extremely," Madison said quietly.

"I will call for a physician immediately –"

"No."

"What's that?" Henry turned back towards her.

"No, I do not need a physician," Madison said more loudly.

"If you are unwell –"

"I do not think that a doctor can fix a broken heart," Madison said, crossing her arms in front of her and glaring defiantly at him across the room.

Henry sighed deeply. He forced himself to cross the room and stand at the edge of her bed. "Don't you think you're being a tad dramatic, love?" He said with a forced smile.

"Do not make light of this! This is our marriage," Madison said angrily.

He opened his mouth to say something else, but then closed it because he had no idea what to say anymore. Whatever Madison wanted out of their marriage, he seemed unable to provide it. Unable to come up with anything to say, Henry took his turn staring out the window aimlessly.

"I met your mistress."

Henry's head snapped back to Madison. She was looking right at him with a good facsimile of her usual confidence. But Henry could see that her lips were quivering and her beautiful golden-green eyes were unusually bright, filled with tears she was just barely holding back.

Henry shook his head: "I don't have a mistress."

"I met her, Henry," Madison said. Henry continued to shake his head. "The Countess of Blyth? She certainly had a lot to say about you."

"Selena is making things up –"

"You do know her!" Madison said, his casual use of the Countess' given name hitting her like a lightning strike straight to the heart.

"Of course, I know her," Henry said automatically. He regretted it instantly as he saw Madison's face fall. "She is not my mistress, not anymore."

Madison shook her head in frustration. "Not anymore," she echoed, her heart and brain trying to process her pain.

Henry could see her beginning to spiral. She wasn't looking at him anymore but staring into the distance. Henry felt a creeping feeling in the pit of his stomach: he was losing her. Desperately he tried to explain: "We were involved, it is true. But we have not been intimate for years. The relationship we have now is strictly financial."

When Madison did not interject or react, Henry plowed on. "Years ago, we went in together on a wine venture. We both invested on a lark. But the business has done very well and we have continued to partner on its expansion and growth. That is the extent of it. We meet and correspond a few times a month about the business. There is nothing more to our relationship than that."

Madison heard every word he said but she could not take it in. She was picturing every romantic, intimate moment she and Henry had shared over the past months … except in her place was the glamorous, mature Countess. As she sat there torturing herself, she felt her heart in her chest: beating, throbbing, breaking.

"Madison, please, say something," Henry said, his voice full of feeling. At any other time, Madison would have been touched by the emotion brimming from each word he said. She would have recognized how hard it was for him to ask her for something, to make himself vulnerable without the shield of his good humor and light-hearted smile. But Madison could not see it.

"I don't believe you," Madison said hollowly.

Her words were like a punch in the gut. Henry shook his head in disbelief. How could this be happening? A month ago, as they stood at the altar exchanging their wedding vows, he had thought his life was perfect. But in a few short weeks, everything had fallen apart.

Henry didn't know what to do. Desperate to reestablish any kind of connection between them, he moved closer to her on the bed and took her hand. He reached up and stroked the side of her face. "Madison, love," he said softly, leaning down to gently kiss her lips.

"Don't kiss me!" She cried, pushing him away and scooting backward towards the headboard of the bed to free herself from his embrace. Her eyes were wide with frustration and humiliation. Henry immediately stood up and stepped away, knowing he had done the wrong thing. Again.

He opened his mouth to apologize, but Madison preempted him. She pointed at the door. "Get out."

Completely at a loss, Henry did as she asked. When he closed the door to his bedroom, it felt painfully final.

"Lord Bowden to see you, my lady," the butler said. He was loath to disturb his mistress; her discontent was known to all of the servants. No one knew exactly what was amiss between Lord and Lady Warsham, but the misery in the great house was palpable. He also knew that Lord Warsham did not have a good opinion of the aforementioned gentleman. "Should I turn him away?"

Madison was holding a newspaper in her hands but was not reading it. It gave the illusion of normalcy, but she was not fooling herself and doubted she was fooling the household staff either. She did not want to see Christopher. She did not want to see anyone. It had taken all of the strength that she had to get herself out of bed, dressed, and into the sitting room this morning. But believe it or not, she owed him a debt of gratitude. Without his help, who knew how much longer her husband would have gone on humiliating her in front of the entire *ton*.

"Please show him in," Madison said, laying aside the unread newspaper. The butler looked skeptical but he said nothing. He nodded and left.

A few minutes later, the door opened and Christopher entered. His waistcoat was unbuttoned, his hair mussed. Madison could not help raising her eyebrows. "You look like hell," she said frankly.

"Good morning to you too," Christopher said. He did not ask her permission as he helped himself to a cup of tea from the tray laid out on one of the small tables. He turned to her questioningly, teapot in hand. "The entire pot has gone cold."

Madison shrugged. "So it has."

Christopher set the teapot back down and came to sit in one of the chairs adjacent to her. He had never seen Madison like this. She was curled up on the sofa, her feet tucked under her and a woven blanket draped over her legs. She was dressed plainly, in a soft gray muslin gown that clearly said she was not planning on entertaining visitors or leaving the house. Her long blond hair was brushed and neatly braided, draped over one shoulder. But there were dark circles under her eyes, and she looked deflated.

He leaned back, crossing his arms against his chest. "I was up all night," he said, waiting to see if that got a reaction. Madison gave him none. "I played cards, which I am not particularly good at. I much prefer billiards. And there was a lot of alcohol involved, but —"

"Christopher, I cannot deal with your ridiculous exploits this morning." Madison kicked her legs out from under her and sat up. She sighed deeply. "If you have not noticed, I am not feeling particularly well."

"I'm not blind," Christopher said. Madison glared at him. "I was up late last night playing cards with Viscount Crimpton," Christopher continued.

"I don't care," Madison said, tossing aside the blanket and standing up.

Christopher ignored her and continued: "Viscountess Crimpton is close friends with the Countess of Blyth." Madison stiffened, but she kept her lips pursed and did not say anything. "It took much longer than I would have liked. The Viscount is an insufferable man. But from everything he says, it seems as if we might have been wrong in our suspicions of your Lord Warsham."

Christopher was a bit surprised when Madison did not react at all. "Viscount Crimpton said that Lord Warsham and the Countess are business partners; the Countess has spoken of it to his wife often. Also … the Countess is currently involved in an affair with a rich German businessman who is staying here in London, and has been for many months," Christopher continued. He expected to see Madison's whole aspect change. But she stood still as a sunbeam, her face unmoved.

"I know." Madison finally said. "Well, at least I know the bit about the business partnership," she amended.

Christopher scoffed aloud: "Of course, being a marquess as rich as Midas isn't enough. Your sainted

Henry also has to be a successful and well-connected businessman," he said bitterly.

Madison did not jump to Henry's defense. Christopher reached out and put a tentative hand on her shoulder. Madison held it for a moment, accepting the small gesture of comfort.

"Isn't this good news?" Christopher asked.

"I suppose it is," Madison acknowledged sadly. "But it does not change things. Henry and I came into this marriage expecting and wanting very different things. The simple truth is that he does not love me." She felt herself start to cry. In a few short months, she had gone from a starry-eyed debutante to a lonely, weeping wife.

"Perhaps you were right about love all along, Christopher," she said.

In a completely uncharacteristic action, Christopher put his arm around her and held her gently as her tears gained speed. "For once, I wish I was not right," he murmured as he patted her back helplessly.

Chapter 20

The next few days were the longest of Henry's life. In a mansion like theirs, it should have been easy enough to avoid another person. But he kept running into Madison everywhere. One morning, she was entering their adjoining sitting room at the same moment he was. Madison had snatched a forgotten scarf from the back of the armchair and disappeared without saying a word to him.

Next, it was the dining room. Henry had taken to having breakfast in his study with the express purpose of not running into Madison. But he thought it would be safe enough to cut through the dining room mid-afternoon on his way to the wine cellar. And there she was, standing at the sideboard with Mrs. Palin, the cook, going over the menus for the next week. That time she ignored him completely, continuing her conversation with Mrs. Palin as if he was not even in the room.

By the time Henry descended the stairs to the ground floor that morning, his nerves were bare. He had skipped the morning meal, intending to leave the house immediately and breakfast at his club. But he promised Theo he would bring the book his father had left him about Irish bloodlines; equine bloodlines, that was. Without thinking much about it, he went through the sitting room, along the alcove of windows that overlooked the courtyard, and into the library.

"I –" he started in surprise when he found the room already occupied.

Madison nearly dropped her teacup. Her entire breakfast was spread in front of her, as well as several periodicals. What on earth was he doing in the library this early in the morning? She had specifically started having her breakfast here because it was the room most geographically opposite from his study and his upstairs apartments.

Henry cleared his throat awkwardly. "I am just getting a book for Theodore," he said. He wondered if she would ignore him again this time. Not taking his eyes off of her, he crossed to the bookshelf where the book was located.

Setting down her tea so she did not spill it belatedly, Madison forced herself to stay seated in the room. She had tried running from him, tried ignoring him, but none of it was making her life any easier. "Will you be at the club all day?" She asked, keeping her voice carefully free of emotion.

"No," he said. Madison felt her heart give a hopeful little jump, but she pushed it back down. "I have one last chance to put my case to the leaders of the opposition before the tax repeal comes to a vote in the House of Commons. I do not know when I will be

back this evening," Henry added, crossing back to the
door with the book in his hand.

Of course, Madison thought to herself. The status
quo had not changed between them.

"I shall see you … when I see you," she said,
picking up her newspaper and feigning disinterest.

Henry knew she was putting up an act but he could
not bring himself to cross the divide between them. "I
suppose so," he said. He bowed his head and then
departed.

Madison listened to the sounds of his footfalls on
the tile floors that ran along the alcove. This was her
life now, she realized. She and Henry may live in the
same house, but their lives were separate. She stared
for a long time at the pile of social invitations which
the butler had brought for her. Madison had been
ignoring them for days. But maybe it was time to re-
engage in the social whirl. Maybe if she pretended like
everything was alright, eventually it would be. She
knew that she was not getting the marriage she
wanted, but perhaps Henry was. Perhaps at least one
of them would be happy. As she began to open the
first invitation, another person entered the library.

"Excuse me, my lady. A note arrived for you a few
minutes ago." The footman held out a silver tray with
a neatly sealed envelope upon it.

Madison did not want to lose her gumption. "Put it
on the table," she said.

The footman looked nervous, but then he added:
"I believe it is from your mother, my lady."

Madison put down the invitation she was holding
and reached for the envelope immediately. The
footman left as soon as she took it, but she did not

notice as she tore it open and her eyes scanned the page.

Slowly, she lowered the short note to her lap. "They are leaving," she said in disbelief.

"You're leaving?" Madison nearly yelled as she entered her mother's bedroom.

Anne looked over in surprise from where she was consulting with Mrs. Miller about the logistics of packing up her personal items. Her face softened when she saw her eldest daughter. "I see Hux thinks you do not need an official introduction, even though you are a marchioness now. I will have a word with him about that." Anne winked and turned back to Mrs. Miller.

"Mother!" Madison said, putting her hands on her hips in frustration. Anne glanced back over at her. This time her eyes lingered, looking her daughter over more closely.

"You are upset," Anne said.

"Obviously." Madison pursed her lips.

Anne chuckled, crossing the room. She looped her arm through Madison's and led her over to the window, where there was a cozy cushioned window seat. "What could you possibly have to be upset about? You are a newlywed," Anne said with a knowing smile.

Madison ignored her mother's innuendo. "You are going back to Sommerfield. Why? The Season isn't even half over."

"You're married, my dear," Anne said simply. Mrs. Miller held up two gowns from across the room. Anne pointed to one, the other Mrs. Miller put into a trunk.

"Only just!" Madison protested. "Besides, you've rented the townhouse for the entire season. Why go back to Sommerfield now?"

"You know your father doesn't like the city. And to be perfectly honest, I've had my fair share of entertainment these past few months. I am more than ready to return to the slower pace of country life," Anne explained. She watched Madison's face, seeing the dark clouds weighing on her. She reached out and cupped her daughter's face in her hands. "Oh darling, I know this isn't what you expected."

For a fraction of a second, Madison thought her mother had figured out why she'd come. A wave of relief swept through her. She'd spent the entire carriage ride from her home to theirs planning what she would say to her mother and father. She had come intending to ask her parents to stay in London a few weeks longer. Barring that, she was ready to admit the disaster her marriage had become and ask to return home with them. But then Anne continued.

"Your childhood is over, my dear. Your father and I are leaving, and for the first time it will just be you and your husband alone here in London," Anne said. Madison opened her mouth to speak, but her mother continued: "You belong with Henry now. You are a wife now, first and foremost. A daughter second."

Madison opened her mouth again to respond, to tell her mother the truth. But instead, the door of the room opened and her father walked in. "Father —" she began.

"You've come to see us off, have you?" Harold said, taking in the idyllic scene of mother and daughter framed in the sunlight. "I am glad you did.

Your mother insisted she would be fine if you were too busy, but I knew that was just big talk."

Anne stood up and smoothed her gown, shaking her head. "That is quite an exaggeration," Anne said, but as she fussed with her hair she discreetly wiped away a rogue tear.

Madison's father scoffed. "But I will take care of her. I always do." He put his arm around her mother's waist and squeezed gently. For just a moment, Anne laid her head on his shoulder, her face hidden against his dark brown waistcoat. Then she straightened up, seeming to draw strength directly from her supportive husband. She turned back to her daughter with a brave smile.

"He is the one insisting we return to Sommerfield, you know," Anne said after her husband departed the room. Madison watched as her mother stared after him, a soft smile on her face. "But when you love someone, their happiness is as important as your own, and inexplicably intertwined."

Anne turned back towards Mrs. Miller, continuing the chores of packing up a household. Madison watched the chaos around her without taking it in. Her mother's words stuck in her head.

Her entire life, Madison had watched her parents' relationship without truly understanding it. What made their love real was not the declarations of love, but the actions. The quiet moments of support that they gave each other; the moments that they gave of themselves without asking for anything in return. Moments like the one she had just witnessed. Moments like this morning, when Madison had sat alone in the library and decided that she wanted to make Henry happy, even if she could not have the marriage she had always envisioned. *Oh god*, she thought to herself. She really did love Henry.

This was so much worse than she had thought an hour ago. She was not just married to an unreformed rake. She was in love with one.

Chapter 21

H enry knocked hard on the door. The evening was brisk, and he shoved his hands into the pockets of his coat while he waited. His mood was foul. The House of Commons had made their decision this morning. While the issue would now be passed on to the House of Lords, Henry knew that the upper chamber of Parliament would not overturn the will of the lower; at least not in this instance. There was little appetite among the lords for further argument on the matter. The more astute members of the government were already turning their minds to how the loss of revenue could be recouped in other ways. Henry felt extremely defeated. The cause he had been investigating and arguing for months was defeated. His marriage was in shambles. So now he stood on the doorstep of the Countess of Blyth.

It was just after dusk. The sky was darkening and the carriages of the fashionable London *ton* were being brought around to take their owners out to their evening entertainments. It was taking longer than usual for the door to be answered. Perhaps he had not estimated the time correctly and Selena had already left for the evening. *No*, he said to himself, gritting his teeth. She liked to arrive fashionably late and make a scene. He knocked again.

Her housekeeper finally opened the door. She had not kept a butler for years. It seemed that her habit had not changed in recent months.

"I need to speak with the Countess immediately."

The housekeeper looked him over. He had a nervous energy about him, like a pile of kindling that might catch fire at any moment. But her mistress had always been especially fond of this particular caller. "Please, come in, my lord." She opened the door to admit him.

Henry did not hesitate. "Where is she?" He asked as he crossed the threshold.

"She is dressing. I will tell her you are here, my lord, if you will wait in the —"

"I will not." Henry cut her off, walking past her and up the stairs of the plush townhouse. Everything was as he remembered it from previous visits. Selena had inherited a great deal of money when her husband died and the evidence of it was all around him. She kept the house and herself in the height of style.

He heard the housekeeper hurrying after him, calling words of reproach once she recovered from her surprise. But Henry ignored her. He turned the corner at the top of the stairs, walked to the end of the hall, and threw open the door to Selena's bedchamber without pause.

"Henry!" Selena said, looking up in surprise from where she was seated at her dressing table. But her face quickly settled into a warm, inviting smile. "What an unexpected and lovely diversion," the Countess said. She stood up slowly, intentionally pulling back her dressing gown as she put her hand to her waist, revealing a long, smooth thigh. With her other hand, she touched her chest suggestively just about her tightly cinched corset. "You will forgive my state of undress. Though it is nothing you have not seen and enjoyed before."

Henry was having none of it. He grabbed the coverlet off the bed and tossed it at her. "Cover yourself up. We need to talk."

Selena caught the coverlet instinctively, but then tossed it to the side without consideration. "You are the one who came into my bedchamber. Remember?" She seated herself on the edge of the bed, leaning back to display her ample breasts. She patted the spot on the bed next to her.

"I will stand," Henry said shortly. "I won't be here long. I have only come to tell you that as of now, our partnership is dissolved. I am selling my interest in the wine business. I will sell it to you if you want it, or I will find another buyer."

"Whatever do you mean? The business has been so profitable." Selena kept her tone light, but she thought she might have a sense of what was coming.

"I don't care. After tonight, I don't intend to ever speak to you again," Henry said. He could feel his anger rising.

Selena sat up. He had her attention now. "Come now, Henry. You cannot be thinking clearly. You are not your usual self at all." She had never seen Henry like this. Serious? Occasionally. Jocular and light-hearted? Almost always. Angry? Never. "Come, have a drink with me and we will talk about this." She motioned for her housekeeper, who had frozen in the doorway, to bring them refreshments.

"You have done enough talking, Selena. I do not want you to talk to my wife ever again." As he talked, Henry paced the room. "What were you thinking, lying to her like that?"

"I did not lie to her—"

"Enough!" Henry slammed his fist down on the armoire beside him. "Enough of your games! You told Madison that you and I were still involved when you knew that was not the truth. You purposefully hurt her." He turned to face her directly, his eyes and voice deadly serious. "Put the word out to all of your nasty, gossiping society friends: my wife is off-limits. Anyone who disrespects her will have me to answer to."

The housekeeper entered the room with a tray holding a bottle of wine and two glasses. Henry laughed, but it did not have the warm musical cadence that he was known for. It was a hard, bitter sound. "Wine, how fitting," he said humorlessly. "Do not speak to my wife or me ever again."

Then he left.

As he mounted his horse, Henry could feel that the weight on him had lifted ever-so-slightly. He should have come here first thing when Madison expressed her concern. *No*, he corrected himself. He should have dissolved his financial arrangement with Selena the moment that Madison had entered his life. Keeping up a relationship, any kind of relationship, with his former mistress was disrespectful to his wife and bound to cause strife at some point.

For the first evening in many, he steered his mount not towards his club, but towards home. He needed to talk to Madison. Henry had no idea what he would say to her. As he moved through the evening bustle of the London streets, he tried to find the words to tell her how he felt. The marriage he had envisioned for them: a cordial relationship centered around social gatherings, a shared but distant existence to keep the houses and estates running … it was not working. It was not making Madison happy. And what Henry had realized over the past few days was that making Madison happy was the most important thing to him.

Do I love her? He asked himself. He tried to say the words aloud. "I love you," he said, first under his breath and then with more veracity. He spoke so loudly that a passerby gave him a strange look. Henry laughed at himself and rode on.

He did not dislike the way it felt on his tongue. But he still was not sure. He had never heard his mother or father say those words to one another, nor to him or his sisters. Perhaps his sisters shared those words with their own husbands, but never in front of Henry. What he felt for Madison surpassed the mutual respect he had witnessed between his parents. He knew that. When he was with her, all he wanted to do was touch her, kiss her, hold her. Henry could not begin to picture his austere father being bothered by his mother's emotions. And yet, when Henry saw how deeply Madison was suffering it was like a knife in his gut.

He had to make amends with her.

He had courted her, wedded her, and bedded her. He cared for her deeply. This rift between them could not go on.

Henry was nearing the mansion. Two more turns, three blocks, and he would be there. Madison had been declining all social engagements. Hopefully, she hadn't changed her mind and gone out tonight or he might miss her.

As he rounded the corner, he had to rein in his horse quickly to prevent him from running into the wagon that was stopped in the middle of the road. Perched high on his horse, and tall as he was, Henry could see some sort of commotion farther down the block. Bystanders were watching from the sides of the street and all four-legged and wheeled traffic had come to a complete stop.

People were yelling in distress. Henry jumped down, handing the reins to a surprised bystander, and began pushing through the crowd. He was heads taller than everyone around him. As he approached the scene, he felt a growing sense of dread taking grip in his stomach. It was full dark now and the only light came from the street lamps that lined the street. The lamplighter must have come down this street before the incident occurred.

An accident, Henry realized as he got closer. The carriage was on its side, the wheels completely useless as they jutted out. The horse that had pulled the carriage was injured. In the darkness, it was hard to see exactly what had happened. But the remnants of a wagon were no more than a pile of rubble in front of the overturned carriage, and the contents it had carried spilled all over the ground.

Henry felt his chest tightening. It was an accident just like this that had taken his parents from him. A meaningless mistake that had left him, a young boy of thirteen, alone with older sisters who were already married and about their own lives. As he moved closer to the carnage, he saw in his mind his parents' funeral, felt the deep sadness that had permeated the weeks and months that followed. He tried to shake it off. He needed to see if he could help.

A woman was crying. She was sitting on the ground next to the wagon sobbing, a man covered in blood draped over her lap. Someone was trying to pry open the carriage door. Inside someone was calling frantically for help. He moved instinctively to lend his strength.

Then Henry recognized the carriage. It was hard to notice in the dark, but the ornate carving along the baseboard was not common. He was rooted to the spot. Images flashed through his mind again, but this time he saw not his parents' funeral, but Madison's. He felt his body spring into action, but his mind was totally dark.

Chapter 22

*M*adison lingered with her parents until the very last moment. She was dreading going home to another tense confrontation with Henry. She helped her mother's maid with packing up Anne's garments and accessories so her mother could supervise the removal of personal items from the rest of the house. When that was finished, Madison went to the bedroom she had occupied in the rented townhouse and looked through the remainder of her items. A handful of things she would send back to Sommerfield with her mother and father. But she directed the majority of the personal items to be sent to Carcliffe Castle, Henry's estate in the country. Her mother said she would send along Madison's remaining wardrobe and possessions back at Sommerfield on to Carcliffe Castle as well.

When they were first getting to know one another, Carcliffe Castle had been an exciting mystery. She had looked forward to going there at the end of the Season to get to know their staff, tenants, and neighbors. While London was the center of the social season, Madison knew well enough that the role she would play as the highest-ranked woman in the county would be equally important. She was sad to admit that it did not hold the same allure now.

As the sun was setting, Madison followed her mother and father outside onto the doorstep. The majority of their possessions would follow them tomorrow. But their carriage stood ready to start the journey homeward immediately.

"Are you sure I cannot convince you to stay another few days?" Madison said wistfully, holding her mother's hand tightly. "It doesn't seem safe to travel at night like this …"

Anne clucked and patted her daughter's hand. "We will be perfectly safe, my dear. The coachman and footman are well prepared for any emergency, and we won't be going more than a few hours on tonight." She leaned over and kissed Madison's cheek. "Congratulations, Madison. You got everything you wanted. You are truly charmed."

Madison thought she saw a tear well up in her mother's eye, but before she could confirm Anne had given her hands a final squeeze and turned to climb up into the carriage. Madison's father pulled her into a tight embrace.

"Don't fret, Maddie. Whatever is bothering you, I know you will work it out. You always do. So single-minded, you are," Harold said with an affectionate chuckle. Madison managed to give him with a small, tumultuous smile, and then he too was gone.

She watched from the doorway as their carriage went down the street, turned, and then disappeared from view. "My lady, are you ready to return home?" Hux said gently from behind her.

Madison nodded. "Yes, thank you Hux. Thank you for everything." On an impulse, she threw her arms around the butler and hugged him. Hux was shocked, and though he very hesitantly returned her hug he looked relieved when she released him and stepped away.

"I will have your carriage brought around now," he said with a quick bow, disappearing before she could embarrass them further.

Madison bit her lip to stop from laughing at his discomfiture. She was a model of decorum as she let Hux hand her up into her carriage and bid him farewell. Madison thought they must be near to home when the carriage lurched to an unexpected stop. She waited for the motion to resume, but when it did not she tapped on the roof of the carriage. "Is everything alright?" She called.

"There is a blockage on the road, madam. An accident of some kind, I think," her driver called down.

Madison opened the door of the carriage and leaned out. Sure enough, she could see a mass of people, carts, wagons, and horses crowding the street. She tried to get a good look, but given her diminutive stature, it was impossible. "We had best go see what is going on. If there was an accident, someone may need help."

The driver and footman exchanged dubious looks, but she was already starting to make her way through the throng of people.

Madison could feel the frenetic energy of the crowd. Small as she was, she was able to slip between people with ease and quickly found herself at the scene of the accident. There was an overturned carriage and wagon in shambles. The door had been ripped from the carriage, and several injured people were being seen to by other individuals; it seemed like medical care was already being dispensed. Not that she could have helped in that department anyway, Madison thought to herself.

But she was good at organizing and commanding a group. She looked over the scene at large, thinking that the next thing to do would be to mobilize some strong-looking men to start clearing the rubble so traffic could start to pass through. As she surveyed the crowd, her eyes froze on a familiar figure.

"Henry?" Madison gingerly climbed over a few large pieces of debris to where her husband stood still as a stone on the edge of the scene. She knew immediately that something was wrong with him. He was white as a sheet, his body rigid. Though she was standing right in front of him, his eyes were not focused on her nor the spectacle in front of them. It was like he was seeing a completely different reality.

"What is going on? Were you in the accident?" Madison asked frantically, checking his body for wounds. She ran her hands urgently along his chest and arms, peering around him to check his back and head. He seemed physically intact. "Henry," she repeated. No response. "Henry!" She said more loudly.

Madison reached down and grabbed his hand, twining his fingers between hers and squeezing hard. "Henry," she whispered, her voice almost begging.

Suddenly, she felt his grip tighten on hers. She looked up quickly and saw his eyes starting to clear. "You were in the accident," he mumbled.

Madison looked back at the scene. It was dark, but she realized immediately what must have happened. The carriage overturned on the ground bore a striking resemblance to their own. And in the dark of the evening, only a few hundred feet from their own home, Henry had drawn a tragic conclusion.

"I am fine, it's not our carriage," Madison said, still gripping his hand tightly. Henry looked confused. She took his other hand and touched it to the side of her face. "I am safe. I am right here."

Henry's breath was coming hard and fast. He seemed to be coming out of his trance, his eyes darting around the scene trying to make sense of everything around them. Madison's heart ached. *His parents died in a carriage accident.* Lord, she could not imagine what he was feeling right now.

Making a quick decision, Madison started to pull on Henry's hand. "Come, Henry." He did not move immediately, but when she kept insisting he allowed her to lead him through the crowd and away from the commotion.

The road cleared as they moved up the block. Madison spotted their footman over her shoulder, walking a few paces behind them. She motioned for him to step back, to give them a little space. She led Henry across the street and into the park. Madison had come here often since their marriage to go for walks with her friend Eve or just to sit by herself on a bench and think. That was where she led Henry, towards a secluded bench in a small stand of trees off the side of the path. It was dark, there was no one about, and through the trees the sounds of the accident and surrounding crowd faded away.

"Wait for us on the street," Madison said over her shoulder to the footman. The young man nodded and turned around, disappearing out of sight. She turned back to Henry, who was staring at her. "Are you alright?" She asked.

Henry nodded his head slowly. When he spoke, his voice was his own and he seemed to have regained himself. "I saw the carriage and I thought you were in the accident."

"Yes, I saw what happened. It was an easy mistake," Madison said sympathetically.

"I was so scared." Henry looked down at his hands. "I pulled the door off the carriage and got the women out. When you weren't there ..." he trailed off. Madison just nodded.

After a while, she said: "I was at my parents' townhouse all day. They have departed for Sommerfield early."

They sat in silence for a long time. Henry was trying to process what had just happened to him. He had felt stress before. Certainly, he had: as a young man losing his parents so early, assuming the responsibilities of a marquess at only thirteen ... he was not a stranger to loss either. But when he thought he had lost Madison, his world had simply broken. He had so much he needed to say to her. "I thought you had left me. That you'd been taken —"

"I did try to leave you." Madison broke in. She saw Henry's eyes darken, heavy confusion and hurt showing on his face. But she rushed on. "When my mother sent word that they were returning to

Sommerfield, I went to their townhouse with every intention of going with them."

As she spoke, Henry's face softened but became more inscrutable. He sighed. Then he asked: "Why didn't you?"

Madison bit her lip to keep it from quivering. "Because I am in love with you," she said, forcing herself to keep her eyes on his even though she was terrified of the rejection she might find there. Henry's brow was furrowed, but in the moonlight, she could not read his expression any more than that. She kept speaking before she lost her nerve. "I have always wanted a love match. I grew up watching my parents' relationship. I thought it was normal. But as I learned more about society, I realized that what they have goes far beyond kind, affectionate regard for one another. They have a true love. And that was the standard I set for myself."

A tear escaped down her cheek. Madison could not look at him any longer. She stared down at her hands, grasped tight together in her lap. "I realize now how foolish and stupid I have been," she said quietly.

Henry's hand closed over hers.

"Then I am foolish and stupid as well."

Madison's head snapped up. He caught her chin in his hand and brought his lips to hers. As he kissed her, his hand slid to the back of her neck, cradling her head and holding her close to him. She was here, she was real, she was alive. His body was aching to confirm what his mind and heart knew. But he had to say the words now or he might never get them out.

He pulled back, keeping his hand tangled in her hair, her face inches from his. "I am in love with you, Madison."

She threw herself into his arms, pulling him tightly against her and kissing him. She took possession of his mouth with her own, kissing him with the passion he had taught her. As he ran his hands over her shoulders and back, Madison moved across the bench so she was in his lap, his body circling hers completely.

Henry started kissing his way along her neck. *She is everything.* The words formed in his mind, and Henry realized there was more he needed to say. With a monumental effort, he pulled himself away from her. Madison looked up at him, questioning and confused.

"I love you, Madison," Henry repeated, letting himself fully feel the words as he said them. "I don't know what that means, or how to do it right. I did not have an example to look at and learn from. I haven't said those words to anyone since well before my parents died. But I do love you."

Madison reached up, tracing his mouth with her fingertips. "I was so afraid I would never hear you say those words," she said, tracing the outline of each lip. "Loving you is the hardest and best thing I have ever done."

"I thought you looked like a moonbeam on our wedding night. And here you are again, like a goddess of the moon saving me from myself." Lifting her in his arms, Henry lowered her gently to the soft grass at their feet.

He slid his fingertips under the clasp of her cloak, unfastening and spreading it on the ground underneath her. Madison's skin rippled in response to the cool night air, but she did not feel cold at all. She reached her hands around his neck and pulled him down to her, arching her hips to meet his as they kissed again.

Henry undressed her slowly, savoring every bit of her as it was revealed to him. Her skin shone in the moonlight. As he peeled away her gown, he left a line of tender kisses along the top of her breasts. He drew her nipple, tight against the cold, into his mouth as his hand slid lower. While the warmth of his mouth teased, he removed all of her undergarments. When he had tossed aside the last piece of fabric, he sat up to look at her.

Madison smiled up at him wickedly. "Your turn," she said, sitting up.

She started with his shoulder, pressing kisses on his hot skin while she unbuttoned and pulled away his shirt. As Madison ran her hands over his stomach and chest, she felt the hard thud of his heartbeat in his chest. For a moment she was completely overcome with love. She rested her forehead on his chest, taking deep breaths. Then the tension released and she could not keep still. She pulled him against her, back towards the ground.

They kissed for a long time, their hands moving over each other's bodies constantly – stroking, caressing, giving, and taking. Finally, neither of them could bear it any longer. When Henry entered her, and they moved as one, the rest of the world fell away.

"Madison," he moaned, reaching for her hand. She caught it and held it tightly, reveling in the connection between every part of their bodies and souls.

Henry listened to every moan, reading her body as it moved against his. When she cried out in bliss, he finally let himself fully relax. He joined her quickly, ecstasy coursing through him.

He lowered himself to the ground, pulling her into his arms. They laid there in the grass, staring up at the stars. The moon had passed from view, leaving them holding tight together in the quiet dark of night. "I love you," Henry said again softly.

Letting the words and feelings and stars wash over her, Madison whispered back: "I love you too."

Epilogue

*O*ne year later...
Henry stood at the window overlooking the courtyard. There had been a steady stream of carriages arriving for a quarter of an hour. His beleaguered staff was scurrying around the courtyard, trying to keep up with the never-ending parade. Henry shook his head unconsciously. This was just the beginning; he doubted the barrage of guests would let up anytime in the next hour. It was not often that the Marquess of Clydon gave a ball. *It hadn't been often,* he corrected himself. Henry suspected now that Madison had the bit between her teeth, she was not going to let go anytime soon. He had never met anyone more perfect for the role of society hostess.

"Tricky little vixen," he muttered under his breath.

"Thinking about me, are you?" Madison said, appearing behind him.

"How'd you know?" Henry asked.

Madison rolled her eyes. "I am not sure if it was the word 'little' or 'vixen' that tipped me off." She stepped forward to look out the window with him and let out a little gasp of surprise. "Look at that."

"Surprised at your success?" Henry raised his eyebrows disbelievingly.

"I am surprised the rest of the *ton* has forgiven you for how rude you were at Lady Sheridan's concert last week."

"I was not rude!"

"You made a very loud comment about how you did not hear a single bar of her daughter's recital," Madison reminded him.

"And whose fault is that?" Henry retorted.

Madison just smiled.

Henry leaned down so his mouth was right behind Madison's ear. "If you do not want me to say embarrassing things about missing debutante's musical recitals, then make an effort to not look so damn delectable that we spend the entire concert defiling Lord Sheridan's study."

Madison shuttered as his warm breath skittered along her skin and his fingertips reached up to touch the nape of her neck. She cleared her throat, trying to get ahold of herself. She twined his fingers in her own to prevent him from exploring further. "Let's go downstairs and greet our guests before we have a repeat performance."

Henry's laughter filled the hallway, warm and engaging. "Fair enough, love. Let us go." He took her hand and led her down the winding staircase towards the grand entry hall of their home. Guests were visible already beginning to fill the floor below. Madison paused on the landing before taking the final handful of stairs. Henry looked at her questioningly.

"I want to take it all in, just for a moment." Madison looked around the hall, with its doors thrown wide open to the grand ballroom beyond. She soaked in the sound of music already beginning to float through the air. She closed her eyes and took a deep breath of the floral arrangements that had been delivered that morning: giant arrangements of white roses and yellow daffodils.

Henry squeezed her hand. "People are starting to stare at us," he said quietly.

Madison chuckled. "Let them stare," she said, looking up at her handsome husband. She knew they made a striking, unique pair. Let their guests admire them and what they had built together. She leaned her head towards her husband, speaking so only he could hear. "So, Henry, do you think you made the right decision, to really give our marriage a go?"

Henry inclined his head. Reaching out with his free hand, he caught her chin with his finger. "I love you, absolutely, Madison," he said as he stared into her shining eyes. "You got exactly what you wanted," he added teasingly.

Madison cocked an eyebrow. "I always get what I want. Haven't you learned that by now?"

Rather than answer that, Henry leaned down and kissed her right there in the entry hall in clear view of all their guests. They garnered many raised eyebrows, and a few guests even shook their heads and whispered disapproving comments to their companions. But neither Henry nor Madison cared. Because after all, theirs was a love match.

Also by Cara Maxwell

The Hesitant Husbands

Racing Rogues

Visit caramaxwellromance.com for previews of upcoming books and special offers. Follow @caramaxwellromance on Instagram for updates and exclusive content.

About the Author

Bringing fresh perspective and punch to the genre readers already know and love, Cara Maxwell is dedicated to writing spirited heroines and irresistible rogues who you will root for every time. A lifetime reader of romance, Cara put pen to paper (or rather, fingers to keyboard) in 2019 and published her first book. She hasn't slowed down from there.

Cara is an avid traveler. As she explores new places, she imagines her characters walking hand-in-hand down a cobblestone path or sharing a passionate kiss in a secluded alcove. Cara is living out her own happily ever after in Seattle, Washington, where she resides with her husband, daughter, and two cats, RoseArt and Etch-a-Sketch.

Printed in Great Britain
by Amazon